THE CAT'S TABLE

THE CAT'S TABLE

Michael Ondaatje

JONATHAN CAPE
LONDON

Published by Jonathan Cape 2011

2 4 6 8 10 9 7 5 3 1

Copyright © Michael Ondaatje 2011

Michael Ondaatje has asserted his right under the Copyright, Designs
and Patents Act 1988 to be identified as the author of this work

Originally published in Canada by McClelland & Stewart Limited, Toronto, and
in the United States by Alfred A. Knopf, a division of Random House Inc., New York

First published in Great Britain in 2011 by
Jonathan Cape
Random House, 20 Vauxhall Bridge Road,
London SW1V 2SA

www.vintage-books.co.uk

Addresses for companies within The Random House Group Limited can be found
at: www.randomhouse.co.uk/offices.htm

The Random House Group Limited Reg. No. 954009

A CIP catalogue record for this book
is available from the British Library

ISBN 9780224093613 (HARDBACK)
ISBN 9780224093620 (TRADE PAPERBACK)

The Random House Group Limited supports The Forest Stewardship Council
(FSC®), the leading international forest certification organisation. Our books carrying
the FSC label are printed on FSC® certified paper. FSC is the only forest certification
scheme endorsed by the leading environmental organisations, including Greenpeace.
Our paper procurement policy can be found at www.randomhouse.co.uk/environment

Typeset in Adobe Garamond by Palimpsest Book Production Limited,
Falkirk, Stirlingshire
Printed and bound in Great Britain by
Clays Ltd, St Ives plc

For Quintin, Griffin, Kristin and Esta

For Anthony and Constance

And this is how I see the East . . . I see it always from a small boat – not a light, not a stir, not a sound. We conversed in low whispers, as if afraid to wake up the land . . . It is all in that moment when I opened my young eyes on it. I came upon it from a tussle with the sea.

JOSEPH CONRAD, 'YOUTH'

THE CAT'S TABLE

HE WASN'T TALKING. HE WAS LOOKING FROM THE window of the car all the way. Two adults in the front seat spoke quietly under their breath. He could have listened if he wanted to, but he didn't. For a while, at the section of the road where the river sometimes flooded, he could hear the spray of water at the wheels. They entered the Fort and the car slipped silently past the post office building and the clock tower. At this hour of the night there was barely any traffic in Colombo. They drove out along Reclamation Road, passed St Anthony's Church, and after that he saw the last of the food stalls, each lit with a single bulb. Then they entered a vast open space that was the harbour, with only a string of lights in the distance along the pier. He got out and stood by the warmth of the car.

He could hear the stray dogs that lived on the quays barking out of the darkness. Nearly everything around him was invisible, save for what could be seen under the spray of a few sulphur lanterns – watersiders pulling a procession of baggage wagons, some families huddled together. They were all beginning to walk towards the ship.

He was eleven years old that night when, green as he could be about the world, he climbed aboard the first and only ship of his life. It felt as if a city had been added to the coast, better lit than any town or village. He went up the gangplank, watching only the path of his feet – nothing ahead of him existed – and continued till he faced the dark harbour and sea. There were outlines of other ships farther out, beginning to turn on lights. He stood alone, smelling everything, then came back through the noise and the crowd to the side that faced land. A yellow glow over the city. Already it felt there was a wall between him and what took place there. Stewards began handing out food and cordials. He ate several sandwiches, and after that he made his way down to his cabin, undressed, and slipped into the narrow bunk. He'd never slept under a blanket before, save once in Nuwara Eliya. He was wide awake. The cabin was below the level of the waves, so there was no porthole. He found a switch beside the bed and when he pressed it his head and pillow were suddenly lit by a cone of light.

He did not go back up on deck for a last look, or to wave at his relatives who had brought him to the harbour. He could hear singing and imagined the slow and then eager parting of families taking place in the thrilling night air. I do not know, even now, why he chose this solitude. Had whoever brought him onto the *Oronsay* already left? In films people tear themselves away from one another weeping, and the ship separates from land while the departed hold on to those disappearing faces until all distinction is lost.

I try to imagine who the boy on the ship was. Perhaps a sense of self is not even there in his nervous stillness in the narrow bunk, in this green grasshopper or little cricket, as if he has been smuggled away accidentally, with no knowledge of the act, into the future.

He woke up, hearing passengers running along the corridor. So he got back into his clothes and left the cabin. Something was happening. Drunken yells filled the night, shouted down by officials. In the middle of B Deck, sailors were attempting to grab hold of the harbour pilot. Having guided the ship meticulously out of the harbour (there were many routes to be avoided because of submerged wrecks and an earlier breakwater), he had gone on to have too many drinks to celebrate his achievement. Now, apparently, he simply did not wish to leave. Not just yet. Perhaps another hour or two with the ship. But the *Oronsay* was eager to depart on the stroke of midnight and the pilot's tug waited at the waterline. The crew had been struggling to force him down the rope ladder, however as there was a danger of his falling to his death, they were now capturing him fishlike in a net, and in this way they lowered him down safely. It seemed to be in no way an embarrassment to the man, but the episode clearly was to the officials of the Orient Line who were on the bridge, furious in their white uniforms. The passengers cheered as the tug broke away. Then there was the sound of the two-stroke and the pilot's weary singing as the tug disappeared into the night.

Departure

WHAT HAD THERE BEEN BEFORE SUCH A SHIP IN MY life? A dugout canoe on a river journey? A launch in Trincomalee harbour? There were always fishing boats on our horizon. But I could never have imagined the grandeur of this castle that was to cross the sea. The longest journeys I had made were car rides to Nuwara Eliya and Horton Plains, or the train to Jaffna, which we boarded at seven a.m. and disembarked from in the late afternoon. We made that journey with our egg sandwiches, some *thalagulies*, a pack of cards and a small Boy's Own adventure.

But now it had been arranged I would be travelling to England by ship, and that I would be making the journey alone. No mention was made that this might be an unusual experience or that it could be exciting or dangerous, so I did not approach it with any joy or fear. I was not forewarned that the ship would have seven levels, hold more than six hundred people including a captain, nine cooks, engineers, a veterinarian, and that it would contain a small jail and chlorinated pools that would actually sail with us over two oceans. The departure date was marked casually on the calendar by my aunt, who had notified the school that I would be leaving at the end of the term. The fact of my being at sea for twenty-one days was spoken of as having not much significance, so I was surprised my relatives were even bothering to accompany me to the harbour. I had assumed I would be taking a bus by myself and then change onto another at Borella Junction.

There had been just one attempt to introduce me to the situation of the journey. A lady named Flavia Prins, whose husband knew my uncle, turned out to be making the same journey and was invited to tea one afternoon to meet with me. She would be travelling in First Class but promised to keep an eye on me. I shook her hand carefully, as it was covered with rings and bangles, and she then turned away to continue the conversation I had interrupted. I spent most of the hour listening to a few uncles and counting how many of the trimmed sandwiches they ate.

On my last day, I found an empty school examination booklet, a pencil, a pencil sharpener, a traced map of the world, and put them into my small suitcase. I went outside and said goodbye to the generator, and dug up the pieces of the radio I had once taken apart and, being unable to put them back together, had buried under the lawn. I said goodbye to Narayan, and goodbye to Gunepala.

As I got into the car, it was explained to me that after I'd crossed the Indian Ocean and the Arabian Sea and the Red Sea, and gone through the Suez Canal into the Mediterranean, I would arrive one morning on a small pier in England and my mother would meet me there. It was not the magic or the scale of the journey that was of concern to me, but that detail of how my mother could know when exactly I would arrive in that other country.

And if she would be there.

I HEARD A NOTE BEING SLIPPED UNDER MY DOOR. IT assigned me to Table 76 for all my meals. The other bunk had not been slept in. I dressed and went out. I was not used to stairs and climbed them warily.

In the dining room there were nine people at Table 76, and that included two other boys roughly my age.

'We seem to be at the cat's table,' the woman called Miss Lasqueti said. 'We're in the *least* privileged place.'

It was clear we were located far from the Captain's Table, which was at the opposite end of the dining room. One of the two boys at our table was named Ramadhin, and the other was called Cassius. The first was quiet, the other looked scornful, and we ignored one another, although I recognised Cassius. I had gone to the same school, where, even though he was a year older than I was, I knew much about him. He had been notorious and was even expelled for a term. I was sure it was going to take a long time before we spoke. But what was good about our table was that there seemed to be several interesting adults. We had a botanist, and a tailor who owned a shop up in Kandy. Most exciting of all, we had a pianist who cheerfully claimed to have 'hit the skids'.

This was Mr Mazappa. In the evening he played with the ship's orchestra, and during the afternoons he gave piano lessons. As a result, he had a discount on his passage. After that first meal he entertained Ramadhin and Cassius and me with tales of his life. It was by being in Mr Mazappa's company, as he regaled us with confusing and often obscene lyrics from songs he knew, that we three came to accept one another. For we were shy and awkward. Not one of us had made even a gesture of greeting to the other two until Mazappa took us under his wing and advised us to keep our eyes and ears open, that this voyage would be a great education. So by the end of our first day, we discovered we could become curious together.

Another person of interest at the Cat's Table was Mr Nevil, a retired ship dismantler, who was returning to England after a patch of time in the East. We sought out this large and gentle man often, for he had detailed knowledge about the structure of ships. He had dismantled many famous vessels. Unlike Mr Mazappa, Mr Nevil was modest and would speak of these episodes in his past only if you knew how to nudge an incident out of him. If he had not been so modest in the way he responded to our barrage of questions, we would not have believed him, or been so enthralled.

He also had a complete run of the ship, for he was doing safety research for the Orient Line. He introduced us to his cohorts in the engine and furnace rooms, and we watched the activities that took place down there. Compared to First Class, the engine room – at Hades level – churned with unbearable noise and heat. A two-hour walk around the *Oronsay* with Mr Nevil clarified all the dangerous and not-so-dangerous possibilities. He told us the lifeboats swaying in mid-air only *seemed* dangerous, and so, Cassius and Ramadhin and I often climbed into them to have a vantage point for spying on passengers. It had been Miss Lasqueti's remark about our being 'in the least privileged place', with no social importance, that persuaded us into an accurate belief that we were invisible to officials such as the Purser and the Head Steward, and the Captain.

I found out unexpectedly that a distant cousin of mine, Emily de Saram, was on the boat. Sadly, she had not been assigned to the Cat's Table. For years Emily had been the way I discovered what adults thought of me. I'd tell her of my adventures and listen to what she thought. She was honest about what she liked and did not like, and as she was older than I was, I modelled myself on her judgements.

Because I had no brothers or sisters, the closest relatives I had while growing up were adults. There was an assortment of unmarried uncles and slow-moving aunts who were joined at the hip by gossip and status. There was one wealthy relative who took great care to remain in the distance. No one was fond of him, but they all respected him and spoke of him continually. Family members would analyse the dutiful Christmas cards he mailed out each year, discussing the faces of his growing children in the photograph and the size of his house in the background that was like a silent boast. I grew up with such family judgements, and so, until I found myself out of their sight, they governed my cautiousness.

But there was always Emily, my 'machang', who lived almost next door for a period of years. Our childhoods were similar in that our parents were either scattered or unreliable. But her home life was, I suspect, worse than mine – her father's business dealings never assured, and their family lived constantly under the threat of his temper. His wife bowed under his rules. From the scarce amount Emily told me, I knew he was a punisher. Even visiting adults never felt safe around him. It was only children, who were in the house briefly for a birthday party, who enjoyed the uncertainty of his behaviour. He'd swing by to tell us something funny and then push us into the swimming pool. Emily was nervous around him, even when he grabbed her around the shoulders in a loving hug and then made her dance with him, her bare feet balanced on his shoes.

Much of the time her father was away at his job, or he simply disappeared. There was no secure map that Emily could rely on, so I suppose she invented herself. She had a free spirit, a wildness I loved, though she risked herself in various adventures. In the end, luckily, Emily's grandmother paid for her to go off to a boarding school in southern India, so she was away from the presence of her father. I missed her. And when she returned for summer holidays, I did not see that much of her, for she'd caught a temporary summer job with Ceylon Telephone. A company car picked her up each morning, and her boss, Mr Wijebahu, would drop her off at the end of the day. Mr Wijebahu, she confided to me, was reputed to have three testicles.

What did bring the two of us together more than anything was Emily's record collection, with all those lifetimes and desires rhymed and distilled into two or three minutes of a song. Mining heroes, consumptive girls who lived above pawnshops, gold diggers, famous cricketers, and even the fact that they had no more bananas. She thought I was a bit of a dreamer, and taught me to dance, to hold her waist while her upraised arms swayed, and to leap onto and over the sofa so it tilted and fell backwards with our weight. Then she would be suddenly away, at school, far away in India again, unheard from, save for a few letters to her mother, where she begged for more cakes to be sent via the Belgian Consulate, letters her father insisted on reading aloud, proudly, to all his neighbours.

By the time Emily came on board the *Oronsay*, I had in fact not seen her for two years. It was a shock to recognise her now as more distinct, with a leaner face, and to be conscious of a grace that I had not been aware of before. She was now seventeen years old, and school had, I thought, knocked some of the wildness out of her, though there was a slight drawl when she spoke that I liked. The fact that she'd grab my shoulder as I was running past her on the Promenade Deck and make me talk with her gave me some cachet among my two new friends on the boat. But most of the time she made it clear she did not wish to be followed around. She had her own plans for the voyage . . . a final few weeks of freedom before she arrived in England to complete her last two years of schooling.

*   *   *

The friendship between the quiet Ramadhin and the exuberant Cassius and me grew fast, although we kept a great deal from one another. At least, this was true of me. What I held in my right hand never got revealed to the left. I had already been trained into cautiousness. In the boarding schools we went to, a fear of punishment created a skill in lying, and I learned to withhold small pertinent truths. Punishment, it turns out, never did train or humble some of us into complete honesty. We were, it seems, continually beaten because of miserable report cards or a variety of vices (lounging in the sanatorium for three days pretending to have mumps, permanently staining one of the school bathtubs by dissolving ink pellets in water to manufacture ink for the senior school). Our worst executioner was the junior school master, Father Barnabus, who still stalks my memory with his weapon of choice, which was a long splintered bamboo cane. He never used words or reason. He just moved dangerously among us.

On the *Oronsay*, however, there was the chance to escape all order. And I reinvented myself in this seemingly imaginary world, with its ship dismantlers and tailors and adult passengers who, during the evening celebrations, staggered around in giant animal heads, some of the women dancing with skirts barely there, as the ship's orchestra, including Mr Mazappa, played on the bandstand all wearing outfits of exactly the same plum colour.

LATE AT NIGHT, AFTER THE SPECIALLY INVITED FIRST Class passengers had left the Captain's Table, and after the dancing had ended with couples, their masks removed, barely stirring in each other's arms, and after the stewards had taken away the abandoned glasses and ashtrays and were leaning on the four-foot-wide brooms to sweep away the coloured swirls of paper, they brought out the prisoner.

It was usually before midnight. The deck shone because of a cloudless moon. He appeared with the guards, one chained to him, one walking behind him with a baton. We did not know what his crime was. We assumed it could only have been a murder. The concept of anything more intricate, such as a crime of passion or a political betrayal, did not exist in us then. He looked powerful, self-contained, and he was barefoot.

Cassius had discovered this late-night schedule for the prisoner's walk, so the three of us were often there at that hour. He could, we thought among ourselves, leap over the railing, along with the guard who was chained to him, into the dark sea. We thought of him running and leaping this way to his death. We thought this, I suppose, because we were young, for the very idea of a *chain*, of being *contained*, was like suffocation. At our age we could not endure the idea of it. We could hardly stand to wear sandals when we went for meals, and every night as we ate at our table in the dining room we imagined the prisoner eating scraps from a metal tray, barefoot in his cell.

I HAD BEEN ASKED TO DRESS APPROPRIATELY BEFORE entering the carpeted First Class Lounge in order to visit Flavia Prins. Though she had promised to keep an eye on me during the journey, to be truthful we would see each other only a few times. Now I had been invited to join her for afternoon tea, her note suggesting I wear a clean and ironed shirt, and also socks with my shoes. I went up to the Verandah Bar punctually at four p.m.

She sighted me as if I were at the far end of a telescope, quite unaware I could read her facial responses. She was sitting at a small table. There followed an arduous attempt at conversation on her part, not helped by my nervous monosyllables. Was I enjoying the voyage? Had I made a friend?

I had made two, I said. A boy name Cassius and another named Ramadhin.

'Ramadhin . . . Is that the Muslim boy, from the cricketing family?'

I said I didn't know but would ask him. My Ramadhin seemed to have no physical prowess whatsoever. He had a passion for sweets and condensed milk. Thinking of this, I pocketed a few biscuits while Mrs Prins was attempting to catch the eye of the waiter.

'I met your father when he was a very young man . . .' she said, then trailed off. I nodded but she said nothing more about him.

'Auntie . . .' I began, feeling secure now in how I could address her. 'Do you know about the prisoner?'

It turned out that she was as eager as I to get away from small talk, and she settled in for a slightly longer interview than she had expected. 'Have more tea,' she murmured, and I did, although I was not enjoying the taste of it. She had heard about the prisoner, she confided, although it was supposed to be a secret. 'He's under very heavy guard. But you must not worry. There's even a very senior British army officer on board.'

I couldn't wait to lean forward. 'I have seen him,' I gloated. 'Walking late at night. Under heavy guard.'

'Really . . .' she drawled, put out by the ace I had played so quickly and easily.

'They say he did a terrible thing,' I said.

'Yes. It is said he killed a judge.'

This was much more than an ace. I sat there with my mouth open.

'An English judge. I should probably not say any more than that,' she added.

My uncle, my mother's brother, who was my guardian in Colombo, was a judge, though he was Ceylonese and not English. The English judge would not have been allowed to preside over a court on the island, so he must have been a visitor, or he could have been brought over as a consultant or advisor. . . Some of this Flavia Prins told me, and some of this I later pieced together with the help of Ramadhin, who had a calm and logical mind.

The prisoner had killed the judge to stop him from helping the prosecution, perhaps. I would have liked to speak to my uncle in Colombo at that very minute. I was in fact feeling worried that his own life might be in danger. *It is said he killed a judge!* The sentence clamoured in my brain. My uncle was a large, genial man. I had been living with him and his wife in Boralesgamuwa since my mother had left for England some years earlier, and while we never had a long or even brief intimate talk, and while he was always busy in his role as a public figure, he was a loving man, and I felt safe with him. When he came home and poured himself a gin he would let me shake the bitters into his glass. I had got into trouble with him only once. He had been presiding over a sensational murder trial involving a cricket player, and I announced to my friends that the suspected man in the dock was innocent, and when asked how I knew, I said that my uncle had said so. I had not said it as a lie so much as something to shore up my belief in this cricketing hero. My uncle, on hearing this, had just laughed casually, but firmly suggested that I not do it again.

Ten minutes after I returned to my friends on D Deck, I was regaling Cassius and Ramadhin with the story of the prisoner's crime. I spoke of it at the Lido pool and I spoke of it around the ping-pong table. But later that afternoon, Miss Lasqueti, who had heard the ripples of my tale, cornered me and made me less certain of Flavia Prins's version of the prisoner's crime. 'He may or may not have done any such thing,' she said. 'Never believe what might be just a rumour.' Thus she made me think that Flavia Prins had dramatised his crime, had raised the bar because I actually had *seen* the prisoner, and so had chosen a crime that I could identify with – the killing of a judge. It would have been an apothecary if my mother's brother had been an apothecary.

That evening I made the first entry in my school examination booklet. A bit of chaos had broken out in the Delilah Lounge when a passenger attacked his wife during a game of cards. Mockery had gone too far during Hearts. There had been an attempt at strangulation and then her ear had been perforated by a fork. I managed to follow the Purser while he guided the wife along a narrow corridor towards the hospital, a dinner serviette staunching the wound, while the husband had stormed off to his cabin.

In spite of the resulting curfew, Ramadhin, Cassius and I slipped from our cabins that night, went along the precarious half-lit stairways, and waited for the prisoner to emerge. It was almost midnight, and the three of us were smoking twigs broken off from a cane chair that we lit and sucked at. Because of his asthma Ramadhin was not enthusiastic about this, but Cassius was eager that we should try to smoke the whole chair before the end of our journey. After an hour it became obvious that the prisoner's night walk had been cancelled. There was darkness all around us, but we knew how to walk through it.

We slid quietly into the swimming pool, relit our twigs and floated on our backs. Silent as corpses we looked at the stars. We felt we were swimming in the sea, rather than a walled-in pool in the middle of the ocean.

THE STEWARD HAD TOLD ME THAT I HAD A ROOMMATE, but so far no one had arrived to take the other bunk. Then, on the third night, while we were still in the Indian Ocean, the lights in the cabin suddenly blazed on, and a man who introduced himself as Mr Hastie entered with a folded-up card table under his arm. He woke me and lifted me onto the top bunk. 'A few friends are coming over for a game,' he said. 'Just go to sleep.' I waited to see who was coming. Within half an hour there were four men playing bridge quietly and earnestly. There was barely enough room for them to sit around the table. They were keeping the volume down because of me, and I soon fell asleep to the whispers of their bidding.

The next morning I found myself alone again. The card table was folded and leaning against the wall. Had Hastie slept? Was he a full-time passenger or a member of the crew? He turned out to be in charge of the kennels on the *Oronsay*, and it must not have been an arduous job, for he spent most of his time reading or half-heartedly exercising the dogs on a small section of deck. As a result, he had energy to burn at the end of the day. So shortly after midnight, his friends joined him.

One of them, Mr Invernio, was his assistant at the kennels. The other two worked on the ship as wireless operators. They played for a couple of hours each night and then left quietly.

I was seldom alone with Mr Hastie. When he turned up at midnight he must have felt I ought to be getting my rest, so he rarely attempted conversation, and there would be only a few minutes before the others arrived. At some stage during his travels in the East, he had picked up the habit of wearing a sarong, and most of the time he wore just that around his waist, even when his friends came by. He'd bring out four shot glasses and some arrack. The bottle and glasses would be placed on the floor, the table cleared of everything except cards. I'd look down from my modest height on the top bunk and see the spread of a dummy hand. I watched the deals, listened to the shuffles and the bidding. *Pass . . . One Spade . . . Pass . . . Two Clubs . . . Pass . . . Two No Trumps . . . Pass . . . Three Diamonds . . . Pass . . . Three Spades . . . Pass . . . Four Diamonds . . . Pass . . . Five Diamonds . . . Double . . . Redouble . . . Pass . . . Pass . . . Pass . . .* They rarely had conversations. I remember they used to call each other by their surnames – 'Mr Tolroy', 'Mr Invernio', 'Mr Hastie', 'Mr Babstock' – as if they were midshipmen in a nineteenth-century naval academy.

Later during the journey, when with my friends I would run into Mr Hastie, he behaved very differently. Outside our cabin, he was opinionated, and a constant talker. He told us about his ups and downs in the Merchant Navy, his adventures with an ex-wife who was a great rider of horses, and his strongly held affection for hounds over any other breed of dog. But in the half-glow of our cabin at midnight, Mr Hastie was a whisperer; he had courteously, after the third evening of cards, replaced the bright yellow cabin light with a muted blue one. So as I entered the realm of half-sleep, drinks were poured, rubbers were won, money changed hands, the blue light making the men seem as if they existed in an aquarium. When they finished their game, the four of them went on deck for a smoke, Mr Hastie slipping back into the room silently half an hour later to read for a while before turning out his bunk light.

SLEEP IS A PRISON FOR A BOY WHO HAS FRIENDS TO meet. We were impatient with the night, up before sunrise surrounded the ship. We could not wait to continue exploring this universe. Lying in my bunk I would hear Ramadhin's gentle knock on the door, in code. A pointless code, really – who else could it have been at that hour? Two taps, a long pause, another tap. If I did not climb down and open the door I would hear his theatrical cough. And if I still did not respond, I would hear him whisper 'Mynah,' which had become my nickname.

We would meet Cassius by the stairs and soon would be strolling barefoot on the First Class deck. First Class was an unguarded palace at six in the morning, and we arrived there even before a fuse of light appeared on the horizon, even before the essential night-lights on the deck blinked and went out automatically at daybreak. We removed our shirts and dived like needles into the gold-painted First Class pool with barely a splash. Silence was essential as we swam in the newly formed half-light.

If we could last undetected for an hour, we had a chance

to plunder the laid-out breakfast on the Sun Deck, heap food onto plates, and abscond with the silver bowl of condensed milk, its spoon standing up in the centre of its thickness. Then we'd climb into the tent-like atmosphere of one of the raised lifeboats and consume our ill-gotten meal. One morning Cassius brought out a Gold Leaf cigarette he had found in a lounge, and taught us how to smoke properly.

Ramadhin politely refused, having his asthmatic condition that was already evident to us and the other diners at the Cat's Table. (As it would continue to be evident when I saw him years later, in London. We were thirteen or fourteen by then, meeting up after losing sight of each other while busy adapting to a foreign land. Even then, when I'd see him with his parents and his sister, Massoumeh, he was constantly catching every neighbourhood cough or flu. We would begin a second friendship in England, but we were different by then, no longer free of the realities of the earth. And in some ways, at that time I was closer to his sister, for Massi always accompanied us on our journeys across South London – to the Herne Hill cycle track, to the Brixton Ritzy, and then the Bon Marché, where we would race down the aisles of food and clothing, for some reason delirious. Some afternoons Massi and I sat on the small sofa in their parents' house in Mill Hill, our hands creeping towards and over each other under the blanket while we pretended to watch the interminable golf coverage on television. Early one morning she came into the upstairs room where Ramadhin and I were sleeping, and sat beside me, her finger to her lips to silence me. Ramadhin asleep in his bed a few feet away. I began to sit up, but she pushed me back with an open palm, then unbuttoned her pyjama shirt so I could see her new breasts, which appeared almost pale green from the reflection of trees outside the window. In the time that followed I was conscious of Ramadhin's cough, the grate as he cleared his throat in his sleep, while Massi, half naked, fearful, fearless, faced me with whatever emotion goes into such a gesture when one is thirteen.)

We left the crockery and the knives and spoons that came with our stolen meals in the lifeboat, and slipped back down to Tourist Class. A steward would eventually discover traces of our numerous breakfasts during a later security drill when the lifeboats were manned and swung over the water, so that for a while the Captain searched for a stowaway on board.

It was not even eight o'clock when we crossed the border from First Class back to Tourist Class. We pretended to stagger with the roll of the ship. I had by now come to love the slow waltz of our vessel from side to side. And the fact that I was on my own, save for the distant Flavia Prins and Emily, was itself an adventure. I had no family responsibilities. I could go anywhere, do anything. And Ramadhin, Cassius and I had already established one rule. Each day we had to do at least one thing that was forbidden. The day had barely begun, and we still had hours ahead of us to perform this task.

WHEN MY PARENTS ABANDONED THEIR MARRIAGE, IT was never really admitted, or explained, but it was also not hidden. If anything it was presented as a mis-step, not a car crash. So how much the curse of my parents' divorce fell upon me I am not sure. I do not recall the weight of it. A boy goes out the door in the morning and will continue to be busy in the evolving map of his world. But it was a precarious youth.

As a young boarder at St Thomas' College, Mount Lavinia, I loved swimming. I loved anything to do with water. On the school grounds there was a concrete channel down which the flood-waters raced during the monsoons. And this became a site for a game some of the boarded boys participated in. We leapt in so we could be hurled forward by the current, somersaulting, flung from side to side. Fifty yards farther along there was a grey rope that we grabbed to pull ourselves out. And twenty yards beyond that, the channel of racing water became a culvert that disappeared underground and journeyed on in darkness. Where it went we never knew.

There might be as many as four of us racing down again and again in the channel waters, one at a time, our heads barely at the surface. It was a nervous game, grabbing the rope, climbing out, then running back under the heavy rain to do it one more time. During one attempt my head submerged as I approached the rope, and I did not come up in time to catch it. My hand was in the air, and that was all as I sped towards the eventual buried culvert. It was my given death, that afternoon in Mount Lavinia, sometime during the March monsoon, foretold by an astrologer. I was nine years old and there would now be a sightless journey into an underground darkness. A hand grabbed my still-raised arm and I was pulled out by an older student. He casually told the four of us off and then hurried away in the rain, not bothering to see if we obeyed him. Who was he? Thank you, I should have said. But I was lying there gasping and drenched on the grass.

What was I in those days? I recall no outside imprint, and therefore no perception of myself. If I had to invent one photograph of myself from childhood, it would be of a barefoot boy in shorts and a cotton shirt, with a couple of friends from the village, running along the mildewed wall that separated the house and garden in Boralesgamuwa from the traffic on the High Level Road. Or it would be of me alone, waiting for them, looking away from the house to the dusty street.

Who realises how contented feral children are? The grasp of the family fell away as soon as I was out the door. Though among ourselves we must have been trying to understand and piece together the adult world, wondering what was going on there, and why. But once we climbed the gangplank onto the *Oronsay*, we were for the first time by necessity in close quarters with adults.

Mazappa

MR MAZAPPA SIDLES UP BESIDE ME, AS I AM EXPLAINING to an ancient passenger the art of unfolding a deckchair in just two moves, links his arm with mine, and makes me walk with him. *'From Natchez to Mobile,'* he warns me, *'from Memphis to Saint Joe . . .'* He pauses at my confusion.

It is always the suddenness of Mr Mazappa's arrival that catches me off guard. As I end a lap in the pool he grips my slippery arm and holds me against the side, crouching there. 'Listen, my peculiar boy, *women will sweet-talk, and give you the big eye . . .* I am protecting you with what I know.' But as an eleven-year-old I do not feel protected, I feel wounded in advance with possibilities. It is worse, even apocalyptic, when he speaks to all three of us. 'When I came home from my last tour, I found a new mule kicking in my stall . . . You know what I mean?' We do not. Until it is explained. Most of the time, though, it is just me he speaks to, as if I am the *peculiar* one on whom an impression can be made. In that regard, he may be right.

Max Mazappa would wake at noon and eat a late breakfast at the Delilah Bar. 'Give me a couple of one-eyed pharaohs, and a Nash soda, will ya,' he'd say, chewing a few cocktail cherries while he waited to be served. After the meal he carried his cup of java to the ballroom piano and placed it on the treble notes. And there, with the piano chords nudging him on, he introduced and educated whoever was with him to the important and complicated details of the world. One day it might be about when to wear a hat, or it could be about spelling. 'It is an *impossible* language, English. *Impossible!* "Egypt", for instance. That's a problem. I'll show you how to spell it right every time. Just repeat the phrase "Ever Grasping Your Precious Tits" to yourself.' And indeed, I never forgot the phrase. Even as I write this now, there is a subliminal hesitation while I capitalise the letters in my head.

But most of the time, he unearthed his musical knowledge, explaining the intricacies of three-quarter time, or recalling some song he had learned from an attractive soprano on a backstage stairway. So we were receiving a sort of feverish biography. *'I took a trip on a train and I thought about you,'* he grumbled, and we thought we were hearing about his sad wasted heart. Though today I realise that Max Mazappa loved the details of structure and melody, for not all of his Stations of the Cross had to do with the failures of love.

He was half Sicilian, half something else, he told us in his un-track-down-able accent. He'd worked in Europe, travelled briefly into the Americas, and gone beyond them until he found himself in the tropics, living above a harbour bar. He taught us the chorus to 'Hong Kong Blues'. He had so many songs and lives under his belt that truth and fiction merged too closely for us to distinguish one from the other. It was easy to fool the three of us, who were naked with innocence. Besides, there were words to some of the songs that Mr Mazappa muttered over the piano keys one afternoon as the ocean's sunlight splashed onto the floor of the ballroom that were unknown to us.

Bitch. Womb.

He was talking to three boys on the verge of pubescence, and he probably knew the effect he was having. But he also imparted to this junior audience stories of musical honour, and the person he celebrated most was Sidney Bechet, who while playing a set in Paris was accused of hitting a false note and in response challenged the accuser to a duel, winged a pedestrian in the fracas that followed, was thrown into jail and deported. 'Le Grand Bechet – Bash – they called him. You boys will live a long, long life,' Mazappa said, 'before you come across such a defence of a principle.'

We were amazed, as well as shocked, by the huge border-less dramas of love that Mazappa's songs and his sighs and confabulations depicted. We assumed that his career's fatal tumble was caused by some deceit or by his too-great love for a woman.

Every month, the changing of the moon.
I say, every month, the changing of the moon,
The blood comes rushing from the bitch's womb.

There was something extraterrestrial and indelible about the verse Mazappa sang on that afternoon, whatever the words meant. We heard it just once, but it remained hidden in us

33

like a stone-hard truth whose bluntness we would continue to veer away from, just as we did then. The verse (by Jelly Roll Morton, I would later discover) was bulletproof and watertight. But we did not know it then, too confused by the directness of it – the words in that last line, its surprising and fatal rhyme, coming so economically after the repetitive opening. We dissolved away from his presence in that ballroom, suddenly aware of stewards up on ladders preparing for the evening's dance, aiming coloured lights, lifting the arches of crêpe paper that criss-crossed the room. They were snapping open the large white tablecloths to drape them over the wooden tables. At the centre of each they positioned a vase of flowers, civilising and romanticising the bare room. Mr Mazappa did not leave with us. He stayed at the piano looking at the keys, unaware of the camouflage taking place around him. We knew that whatever he would be playing with the orchestra that night would not be what he had just been playing for us.

*

MAX MAZAPPA'S STAGE NAME – OR HIS 'WAR NAME', AS he called it – was Sunny Meadows. He began using it after a printing error on a poster advertising his performance in France. Perhaps the promoters had wished to avoid the Levantine quality of his name. On the *Oronsay*, where his piano class was announced in the ship's bulletin, he was also referred to as 'Sunny Meadows, Master of the Piano'. But he was Mazappa to us at the Cat's Table, for *sunny* and *meadows* were hardly words that could exist alongside his nature. There was not much that was optimistic or well trimmed about him. Yet his passion for music invigorated our table. He spent one whole lunch regaling us with that duel of 'Le Grand Bechet', which had ended up more like a gun battle in the early hours of Paris in 1928 – Bechet firing his pistol in the direction of McKendrick, the bullet grazing his accuser's Borsalino, then continuing until it embedded itself in the thigh of a Frenchwoman on her way to work. Mr Mazappa acted it all out, using salt and pepper shakers and a piece of cheese to depict the trajectory of the bullet.

He invited me one afternoon to his cabin to listen to some records. Bechet, Mazappa told me, used the Albert System clarinet, which had a formal and luxurious tone. 'Formal and luxurious,' he kept repeating. He put on a 78 and whispered alongside the music, pointing out the impossible descants and swaggers. 'You see, he *shakes* the sound out.' I did not understand, but was in awe. Mazappa signalled to me each time Bechet made the melody reappear, 'like sunshine on a forest floor', I remember him saying. He fumbled within a waxy-looking suitcase, brought out a notebook, and read what Bechet had told a student. *'I am going to give you one note today,'* Bechet had said. *'See how many ways you can play the note – growl it, smear it, flat it, sharp it, do anything you want to it. It's like talking.'*

Then Mazappa told me about the dog. 'It used to come on stage with Bash and growl when his master was playing . . . And *this* is why Bechet broke up with Duke Ellington. The Duke wouldn't allow Goola up there, in the lights, upstaging his white suit.' So, because of Goola, Bechet left Ellington's band and opened the Southern Tailor Shop, a repair and cleaning operation, as well as a hangout for musicians. 'This was when his best recordings were done – like "Black Stick", "Sweetie Dear". Someday you are going to have to buy all those records.'

And then the sexual life. 'Oh, Bash was a repeater, often ending up with the same woman. . . Women of all kinds attempted to discipline him. But you know, he had been on the road playing since he was sixteen, he had already met girls of every clime and purpose.' Every clime and purpose! *From Natchez to Mobile . . .*

I listened, nodding with incomprehension, while Mr Mazappa clutched to his heart this example of a way of life and musical skill as if they were held inside the oval portrait of a saint.

C Deck

I SAT ON MY BUNK LOOKING AT THE DOOR AND THE metal wall. It was hot in the cabin by late afternoon. I could be alone only if I came here, at this time. Most of my day was busy with Ramadhin and Cassius, sometimes Mazappa or others from the Cat's Table. At night I was often surrounded by the whispering of my card-players. I needed to think backwards for a while. Thinking backwards I could remember the comfort of being curious and alone. After a while I would lie back and look at the ceiling a foot or two above me. I felt safe, even if I was in the middle of the sea.

Sometimes, just before darkness, I found myself on C Deck when no one else was there. I'd walk to the railing, which was the height of my chest, and watch the sea rush alongside the ship. At times it appeared to rise almost to my level, as if wishing to pluck me away. I would not move, in spite of this havoc of fear and aloneness in me. It was the same emotion I had when lost in the narrow streets of the Pettah market, or adapting to new, undiscovered rules at school. When I could not see the ocean, the fear was not there, but now the sea rose in the half-dark, surrounding the ship, and coiled itself around me. No matter how scared I was, I remained there, adjacent to the passing darkness, half wanting to pull myself back, half desiring to leap towards it.

Once, before I left Ceylon, I saw an ocean liner being burned at the far end of Colombo harbour. All afternoon I watched the blue acetylene cut into the flanks of the vessel. I realised the ship I was now on could also be cut into pieces. One day, seeing Mr Nevil, who understood these things, I tugged at his sleeve and asked him if we were safe. He told me the *Oronsay* was healthy, it was only in mid-career. It had worked as a troop ship during the Second World War, and somewhere along one wall of the hold there was a large mural in pink and white of naked women astride gun mounts and tanks that had been painted by a soldier. It was still there, a secret, for the officers on the ship never went into the hold.

'But are we all right?'

He sat me down and, on the back of one of the blueprints he always carried, drew me what he said was a Greek warship, a trireme. 'This was the greatest ship of the seas. And even it no longer exists. It fought the enemies of Athens and brought back unknown fruits and crops, new sciences, architecture, even democracy. All that because of this ship. It had no decoration. The trireme was what it was – a weapon. On it were just rowers and archers. But not even a fragment of one exists now. People still search for them in the silt of river coasts, but they have never found one. They were made out of ash and hard elm, with oak for the keel, and green pine they bent into the shape of the frame. The planks were sewn together with linen cords. There was no metal on the skeleton. So the ship could be burned on a beach, or if it sank, it dissolved in the sea. Our ship is safer.'

For some reason Mr Nevil's depiction of an old warship gave me comfort. I no longer imagined myself on the decorated *Oronsay*, but on something more self-sufficient, more stripped down. I was an archer or a rower, on a trireme. We would enter the Arabian Sea and then the Mediterranean that way, with Mr Nevil as our naval commander.

That night I woke suddenly with the feeling that we were passing islands, and that they were nearby in the darkness. There was a different sound to the waves beside the ship, a sense of an echo, as if they were responding to land. I turned on the yellow light by my bed and looked at the map of the world I had traced from a book. I had forgotten to put names on it. All I knew was that we were going west and north, away from Colombo.

An Australian

IN THE HOUR BEFORE DAWN WHEN WE GOT UP TO roam what felt like a deserted ship, the cavernous saloons smelled of the previous night's cigarettes, and Ramadhin and Cassius and I would already have turned the silent library into a mayhem of rolling trolleys. One morning we suddenly found ourselves hemmed in by a girl on roller skates racing round the wooden perimeter of the upper deck. It seemed she had been getting up even earlier than we had. There was no acknowledgement on her part of our existence as she raced faster and faster, the fluent strides testing her balance. On one turn, mistiming a cornering leap over cables, she crashed into the stern railing. She got up, looked at the slash of blood on her knee, and continued, glancing at her watch. She was Australian, and we were enthralled. We had never witnessed such determination. None of the female members of our families behaved this way. Later we recognised her in the pool, her speed a barrage of water. It would not have surprised us if she'd leapt off the *Oronsay* into the sea and kept pace for twenty minutes alongside the ship.

We therefore began waking even earlier to watch her

roller-skate the fifty or sixty laps. When she was finished, she'd unlace her skates and walk exhausted, sweating and fully clothed, towards the outdoor shower. She would stand in the gush and spray of it, tossing her hair this way, that way, like some clothed animal. This was a new kind of beauty. When she left we followed her footprints, which were already evaporating in the new sunlight as we approached them.

Cassius

WHO WOULD NAME A CHILD CASSIUS, I THINK NOW. Most parents have veered from giving a firstborn such a name. Though Sri Lanka has always enjoyed the merging of classical first names with Sinhalese last names – Solomon and Senaka are not common, but they exist. The name of our family paediatrician was Socrates Gunewardena. In spite of its bad Roman press, Cassius *is* a gentle and whispering name, though the youthful Cassius I got to know on the voyage was very much an iconoclast. I never saw him side with anyone in power. He drew you into his perspective of things and you saw the layers of authority on the ship through his eyes. He relished, for instance, being one of the insignificants at the Cat's Table.

When Cassius spoke about St Thomas' in Mount Lavinia it was with the energy of someone remembering a resistance movement. Since he was a year ahead of me at the school, it felt we were worlds apart, but he was a beacon to the younger students, for he had seldom been caught for his crimes. And when he was caught, not one hint of embarrassment or humility crossed his face. He was especially celebrated after he managed to lock 'Bamboo Stick' Barnabus, our boarding-house master, in the junior school toilet for several hours to protest the revolting lavatories at the school. (You squatted over the hole of hell and washed yourself afterwards with water from a rusty tin that once held Tate & Lyle golden syrup. 'Out of the strong came forth sweetness', I would always remember.)

Cassius had waited until Barnabus entered the students' ground-floor toilet at six a.m. for his habitually long stay, and then, having jammed a metal rod against the door, proceeded to encase the lock with a quick-drying cement. We listened to our housemaster throwing himself against the door. Then he called our names, beginning with the students he trusted. One by one we offered to go for help, then drifted off onto the school grounds, where we had to relieve ourselves behind bushes, and then went for a swim or dutifully entered the seven a.m. homework study class that Father Barnabus had in fact instituted earlier in the term. The cement had to be shattered off with a cricket stump by one of the groundsmen, but that was not until late afternoon. By then we hoped our housemaster would be overcome by fumes, perhaps be faint and uncommunicative. But his vengeance proceeded rapidly. Whipped, then expelled for a week, Cassius became even more of an icon for the junior school, especially after a stirring speech by the Warden at morning chapel that damned him for a full two minutes as if he were one of the fallen angels. Of course, no lesson was learned from this episode – by anyone. Years later when an old boy donated funds to St Thomas' for a new cricket pavilion, my friend Senaka said, 'First they should construct some decent bogs.'

Like me, in order to be accepted into an English school,

Cassius had taken an exam overseen by the Warden. We had to answer several mathematical questions based on pounds and shillings, whereas all we knew were rupees and cents. There were also general-knowledge questions, such as how many men were on the Oxford rowing team and who had lived at a place called Dove Cottage. We were even asked to name three members of the House of Lords. Cassius and I were the only students in the Warden's living room that Saturday afternoon, and he threw me an incorrect answer to the question, 'What do you call a female dog?' He had said, 'Cat,' and I had written that down. It was the first time he had actually spoken to me, and it was with a lie. I had known him until then only by reputation. All of us in the junior school saw him as the incorrigible of St Thomas' College. No doubt it galled the school staff that he would now be representing its name abroad.

There was a mix of stubbornness and kindness in Cassius. I never knew where these qualities came from. He never referred to his parents, and if he had he would probably have invented a scenario to make himself distinct from them. In fact, during the journey the three of us had no real interest in one another's background. Ramadhin would speak now and then of the careful advice his parents had given him about his health. And as for me, all the other two knew was that I had an 'aunt' in First Class. It had been Cassius who recommended we keep our backgrounds to ourselves. He liked the idea, I think, of being self-sufficient. That is how he saw our little gang existing on the ship. He put up with Ramadhin's domestic anecdotes because of his physical weakness. There was a gentle democracy in Cassius. In retrospect, he was only against the power of Caesar.

I suppose he changed me during those twenty-one days, persuading me to interpret anything that took place around us with his quizzical or upside-down perspective. Twenty-one days is a very brief period in a life, but I would never unlearn the whisper of Cassius. As the years went by I would hear of him or read about his career, but I would never meet him again. It was Ramadhin I would keep in touch with, visiting him in Mill Hill, where his family lived, going to matinee movies with him and his sister, or to the Boat Show in Earls Court, where we would try to imagine the deeds that Cassius would commit if he were in our company.

*'Don't look at him, you hear me? Celia? Don't ever look
at the swine again!'*

*'My sister has a strange name. Massoumeh. It means
"immaculate", "protected from sins". But it can also mean
"defenceless".'*

*'I have a specific dislike, I am sorry to say, of the
Sealyham terrier.'*

'I thought she was a bluestocking, at first.'

'We use fruit as a fish poison sometimes.'

'Pickpockets always come out during a storm.'

*'This man said he could cross a desert eating just a
date and one onion a day.'*

*'I suspect, because of her language skills, she was
scooped up by Whitehall.'*

'I'm ruined by that singleton!'

*'I told your husband when he offered me a three-
day-old oyster that it was more dangerous to me than
having a sexual act when I was seventeen.'*

The Hold

LARRY DANIELS WAS ONE OF THOSE WHO ATE WITH US at the Cat's Table. A compact, well-muscled man, he always wore a tie, always had his sleeves rolled up. Born to a burgher family in Kandy, he had become a botanist and spent much of his adult life studying forest and plant cultures in Sumatra and Borneo. This was to be his first journey to Europe. Initially the only thing we knew about him was that he had an over-whelming crush on my cousin Emily, who would barely give him the time of day. Because of this lack of interest he had gone out of his way to befriend me. I suppose he had seen me laughing with her and her friends by the pool, which was where Emily could usually be found. Mr Daniels asked me if I would like to see his 'garden' on the ship. I suggested I bring my two cohorts, and he agreed, though it was clear he wanted me to himself so he could quiz me about my cousin's likes and dislikes.

Whenever Cassius and Ramadhin and I were with Mr Daniels, we'd spend the time asking him to buy us exotic cordials at the pool bar. Or we'd persuade him to make up a foursome at one of the games on deck. He was an intelligent, curious man, but we were more interested in testing our strength by wrestling with him, all three of us attacking him simultaneously, then leaving him gasping on a jute mat while we ran off, sweating, to dive into the pool.

It was only at dinner that I was unprotected from Mr Daniels's queries about Emily, for my assigned seat was next to his, and I would have to talk about her and nothing else. The one piece of information I could honestly give him was that she liked Player's Navy Cut cigarettes. She had been smoking the brand for at least three years. The rest of her likes and dislikes I invented.

'She likes the ice creams at Elephant House,' I said. 'She wishes to go into the theatre. To be an actress.' Daniels grasped at that false straw.

'There's a theatrical company on the ship. Perhaps I could introduce her . . .'

I nodded, as if recommending it, and the next day I saw him speaking to three members of the Jankla Troupe, entertainers on their way to Europe to perform their brand of street theatre and acrobatics, but they were also giving occasional performances for passengers during the journey. They would juggle, sometimes casually at the end of an afternoon tea with their plates and cups, but most of the time they appeared formally, in full costume and excessive make-up. Best of all, they would call passengers up to the improvised stage in order to reveal private things about them, which were sometimes embarrassing. Mostly the revelations involved the location of a lost wallet or ring, or the fact that the passenger was going to Europe to be with a relative who was ill. These things were announced by The Hyderabad Mind, whose face was streaked with purple and whose eyes, rimmed with white paint, looked as if they might have belonged to a giant. Really, he could terrify us, for he would stroll into the depths of the audience to pronounce the number of children a person had, or where his wife had been born.

Late one afternoon, wandering alone on C Deck, I saw The Hyderabad Mind crouching under a lifeboat, putting on his make-up before a performance. He was holding a small mirror in one hand, while the other quickly gashed on stripes of purple paint. The Hyderabad Mind had a slight body, so that the painted head seemed too big for his delicate frame. He peered into the mirror, unaware of me a few feet away as he improved himself in the half-shadow of the lifeboat that hung from the davits. Then he stood, and as he stepped into sunlight the colours burst forward, the ghoulish eyes now full of sulphur and perception. He glanced at me and walked past as if I were nothing. I had witnessed for the first time what possibly took place behind the thin curtain of art, and it gave me some protection the next time I saw him onstage, decked out in full costume. I felt I could almost see, or at least now was aware of, the skeleton within.

It was Cassius who loved the Jankla Troupe most. He was eager to join as a member, especially after Ramadhin called us over excitedly one day to say he had seen one of the troupe remove a watch from the wrist of a man he was giving directions to. It was so subtle the passenger was completely unaware of the loss. Two afternoons later, The Hyderabad Mind strolled into the audience and told the man where his watch 'might' be if he happened to be missing it. This was brilliant.

An earring, a valise, the typewriter from a stateroom were lifted and then fenced to The Hyderabad Mind, and eventually their locations revealed to the owners. When we told Mr Daniels about our discovery, he simply laughed and said it was similar to the art of fly-fishing.

But before Mr Daniels had known about this aspect of the troupe, he simply introduced himself to its members, and said he had a good friend, Miss Emily de Saram, a very talented young lady who loved the theatre, and perhaps she could watch them rehearse if he brought her along? Which he eventually did, I gather, a day or two later, although how much interest in theatre Emily had, I do not know. In any case, this was how she met The Hyderabad Mind and how she went on to live a life different from the one that was expected.

Apart from what we clearly saw as his softness towards Emily, we were not that curious about Mr Daniels. Although nowadays I would probably enjoy the man, would want to walk through some botanical garden of his, listening to him speak of the unusual qualities of a plant we were passing, the fronds and palms and hedgerows brushing our arms.

One afternoon he gathered the three of us and took us where he had promised – into the bowels of the ship. We went through a foreroom where there was a rush of air from two turbine fans linked with the engine room. Mr Daniels had a key, and with it we entered the hold – a cave of darkness that disappeared down several levels into the ship. In the distance below us we could make out a few lights. We climbed down a metal ladder attached to the wall, going by levels full of crates and sacks and giant slabs of raw rubber with its intoxicating smell. We heard the loud croaking purr of a chicken run and laughed at the birds' sudden silence when they became aware of us. We heard rushing water in the walls, which Mr Daniels explained was water being de-salinated after being drawn out of the sea.

Reaching the bottom level of the hold, Mr Daniels set off into the darkness. We followed a path of dim lights that hung just above our heads. He turned right after about fifty yards, and there we came upon the mural Mr Nevil had told me about, of women astride gun barrels. I was startled by its size. The figures were twice as big as we were, and they were smiling and waving though they had no clothes on and the landscape behind them was desert. 'Uncle . . .' Cassius kept asking, 'what is that?' But Mr Daniels would not let us pause and herded us on.

Then we saw a golden light. It was more than that. As we came closer it was a field of colours. This was the 'garden' Mr Daniels was transporting to Europe. We stood in front of it, and then Cassius and I and even Ramadhin began racing through the narrow aisles, leaving Mr Daniels behind in a crouch, studying a plant. How big was this garden? We were never certain, because not all of it was ever fully lit at the same time, for the grow lights that simulated sunshine turned on and off independently. And there must have been other sections we never saw during that journey. I don't even recall its shape. It feels now as if we dreamt it, that it possibly did not exist at the end of that ten-minute walk in the darkness of the hold.

Now and then a mist filled the air, and we would raise our faces to receive the fine rain. Some plants were taller than we were. Some were titchy things no higher than our ankles. We put our arms out and patted the ferns as we passed them.

'Don't touch!' Mr Daniels said, pulling down my out-stretched hand. 'That's *Strychnos nux vomica*. Be careful – it has an alluring smell, especially at night. It almost tempts you to break open that green shell, doesn't it? It looks like your Colombo *bael* fruit, but it isn't. It's a strychnine. These with their flowers facing down are angel's trumpet. The ones facing up, wickedly beautiful, are devil's trumpet. And here's *Scrophulariaceae*, the snapdragon, also deceptively attractive. Even if you just sniff these, you will feel woozy.'

Cassius inhaled deeply and staggered back dramatically and 'passed out', crushing a few frail herbs with his elbow. Mr Daniels went over to move his arm away from an innocent-looking fern.

'Plants have remarkable powers, Cassius. This one's juice keeps your hair black and your fingernails growing at a healthy rate. Over there, those blue ones—'

'A garden on a ship!' Mr Daniels's secret had impressed even Cassius.

'Noah . . .' said Ramadhin quietly.

'Yes. And remember, the sea is also a garden, a poet tells us. Now, come over here. I think I saw the three of you smoking bits of that cane chair the other day . . . This will be better for you.'

He bent down and we crouched with him while he plucked some heart-shaped leaves. 'These are *Piper* betel leaves,' he said, placing them on my open palm. He moved on, picked up some slaked lime from a cache and combined it with slivers of areca nut he had in a jute bag, and handed the mixture to Cassius.

Within minutes we were proceeding along that modestly lit path chewing betel. We were familiar with the mild street intoxicant. And as Mr Daniels had pointed out, it was safer for Ramadhin than smoking a cane chair. 'If you go to a wedding, they sometimes add a sliver of gold to the cardamom and lime paste.' He gave us a small hoard of these ingredients, along with some dehydrated tobacco leaves, which we decided to save for our predawn strolls, when we could spit the red fluid over the railings into the rushing sea or down into the darkness of the foghorns. The three of us walked with Mr Daniels along the various paths. We had been at sea for days, and the range of colours had been limited to white and grey and blue, save for a few sunsets. But now, in this artificially lit garden, the plants exaggerated their greens and blues and extreme yellows, all of them dazzling us. Cassius asked Mr Daniels for more details about poisons. We were hoping he might tell us about a herb or a seed that could overpower an unlikeable adult, but Mr Daniels would say nothing about such things.

We left the garden and returned through the blackness of the hold. When we passed the mural of naked women, Cassius once again asked, 'What is *that*, Uncle?' Then we climbed the metal ladder back to deck level. It was more difficult going up. Mr Daniels was almost a flight above us, and by the time we got to the top he was outside smoking a beedi that was rolled in white paper rather than a brown leaf. He stood with it cupped in his left hand and seemed suddenly keen to lecture us about palms from all over the world. He imitated how they stood and how they swayed, depending on heritage or breed, how they would bend with the wind in their submissiveness. He kept showing us the various palm postures until he had us laughing. Then he offered us the cigarette and demonstrated how to inhale it. Cassius had been eyeing it, but Mr Daniels gave it first to me and the beedi went back and forth among us.

'Unusual beedi,' Cassius said slowly.

Ramadhin took a second puff and said, 'Do the palm trees again, Uncle!' And Mr Daniels proceeded to distinguish for us more of the various postures. 'This of course is the talipot, the umbrella palm,' he said. 'You get your toddy from it, and jaggery. She moves this way.' Then he imitated a royal palm from the Cameroons, which grew in freshwater swamps. Then something from the Azores, followed by a slender-trunked one from New Guinea, his arms becoming its elongated fronds. He compared how they shifted in the wind, some fussily, some with just a sidelong twist of the trunk, so they could face the strongest winds with their narrowest edge.

'Aerodynamics . . . *very* important. Trees are smarter than humans. Even a lily is better than a human. Trees are like whippets . . .'

We were laughing and laughing at all the poses he struck. But suddenly the three of us ran away from him. We screamed as we raced through the women's badminton semi-finals, and leapt cannonballing, with all our clothes on, into the swimming pool. We even got out and dragged a few deckchairs back in with us. It was the popular hour, and mothers with infants were trying to avoid us. We released all the breath from our bodies and sank to the bottom and stood there waving our arms softly like Mr Daniels's palm trees, wishing he could see us.

The Turbine Room

WE NEEDED TO STAY UP TO WITNESS WHAT TOOK PLACE on the ship late at night, but we were already exhausted from waking before sunrise. Ramadhin proposed we sleep in the afternoons, as we had done as children. At boarding school we had scorned these afternoon naps, but now we saw that they might be useful. However, there were problems. Ramadhin was billeted next to a cabin where, he claimed, a couple were laughing and groaning and screeching during the afternoons, while the cabin next to mine was occupied by a woman who practised the violin, the sound easing its way through the metal wall into my room. Just screeching, I said, no laughing. I could even hear her argue with herself between the impossible-to-ignore squawks and plucks. As well, the temperature in these lower cabins that had no portholes was horrific. Any anger I had towards the violin player was modified by knowing that she was also probably perspiring, and likely wearing the bare minimum to be respectable to herself. I never saw her, had no knowledge of what she looked like, or of what she was trying to perfect with that instrument. These did not seem to be Mr Sidney Bechet's 'formal and luxurious' notes. She was just repeating the notes and runs endlessly, then hesitating, and beginning again, with that film of sweat on her shoulders and arms as she spent those afternoons alone, so busy, in the cabin next to mine.

We three were also missing one another's company. In any case, Cassius felt we needed a permanent headquarters, so we chose the small turbine room we'd entered before our descent into the hold with Mr Daniels. And it was here, in the semi-darkness and coolness, with a few blankets and some borrowed lifejackets, that we created a nest for ourselves during some of the afternoons. We would chat for a bit and then sleep soundly in the midst of the loud roar of those fans, preparing ourselves for the long evenings.

But our night investigations were not successful. We were never sure of what we were witnessing, so that our minds were half grabbing the rigging of adult possibility. On one 'night watch' we hid in the shadows of the Promenade Deck and at random followed a man, just to see where he was going. I recognised him as the performer who dressed up as The Hyderabad Mind, whose name we had been told was Sunil. Somewhat surprisingly, he led us to Emily, who was leaning against a railing, wearing a white dress that seemed to glow as he went closer. The Hyderabad Mind half covered her, and she held his fingers cupped within her hands. We could not tell if they were talking.

We stepped back, further into the darkness, and waited. I saw the man move the strap of her dress and bring his face down to her shoulder. Her head was back, looking up at the stars, if there were stars.

THE THREE WEEKS OF THE SEA JOURNEY, AS I ORIGINALLY remembered it, were placid. It is only now, years later, having been prompted by my children to describe the voyage, that it becomes an adventure, when seen through their eyes, even something significant in a life. A rite of passage. But the truth is, grandeur had not been added to my life but had been taken away. As night approached, I missed the chorus of insects, the howls of garden birds, gecko talk. And at dawn, the rain in the trees, the wet tar on Bullers Road, rope burning on the street that was always one of the first palpable smells of the day.

Some mornings in Boralesgamuwa, I used to wake early and make my way through the dark, spacious bungalow until I came to Narayan's door. It was not yet six o'clock. I waited until he came out, tugging his sarong tighter. He'd nod to me, and within a couple of minutes we'd be walking quickly and in silence across the wet grass. He was a very tall man, and I was a boy of eight or nine. Both of us were barefoot. We approached the wooden shack at the foot of the garden. When we were inside, Narayan lit a stump of candle and then crouched

with the yellow light and pulled the cord that burst the generator into life.

So my days began with the muffled shaking and banging
of this creature that gave off the delicious smell of petrol and
smoke. The habits and weaknesses of the generator, circa 1944,
were understood only by Narayan. Gradually he calmed it and
we'd go into the open air, and in the last of the darkness, I'd
see lights go on haltingly all over my uncle's house.

The two of us walked through a gate onto the High Level
Road. A few stores were already open, each lit by a single bulb.
At Jinadasa's we bought egg hoppers, and ate them in the
middle of the almost deserted street, cups of tea at our feet.
Bullock carts heaved by, creaking, their drivers and even the
bullocks half asleep. I always joined Narayan for this dawn
meal after he awakened the generator. Breakfast with him on
the High Level Road was not to be missed, even though it
meant I would have to consume another, more official breakfast
with the family an hour or two later. But it was almost heroic
to walk with Narayan in the dissolving dark, greeting the
waking merchants, watching him bend to light his beedi on a
piece of hemp rope by the cigarette stall.

Narayan and Gunepala, the cook, were my constant companions when I was a child, and I probably spent more time
with them than with my family and learned much from them.
I watched Narayan loosen the blades from a lawnmower in
order to sharpen them, or oil the chain on his bicycle tenderly
with his open palm. Whenever we were in Galle, Narayan and
Gunepala and I would climb down the ramparts to the sea
and swim out so they could fish on the reef for dinner. Late

59

in the evening I'd be found asleep at the foot of my ayah's bed and have to be carried by my uncle to my room. Gunepala, who could be bitter and short-tempered, was a perfectionist. I'd watch him pick out any questionable food from a boiling pot with his calloused fingers and fling it ten feet away into the flower beds – a chicken bone or an overripe *thakkali*, which would be eaten instantly by the rice hounds that hovered about, knowing this habit of his. Gunepala argued with everyone – shopkeepers, lottery ticket salesmen, inquisitive policemen – but he was aware of a universe invisible to the rest of us. As he cooked he whistled a variety of birdcalls rarely heard in the city, familiar to him from his childhood. No one else had that particular focus on what was or could be audible to us. One afternoon he woke me from a deep sleep, took me by the hand, and made me lie down beside some bullock manure on the driveway that had been there for several hours. He pulled me right down beside it and made me listen to the insects *inside* the shit, consuming this feast and tunnelling from one end of the faeces to the other. In his spare time he taught me alternative verses to popular *bailas* that were full of obscenities, swearing me not to repeat them, as they referred to well-known gentry.

Narayan and Gunepala were my essential and affectionate guides during that unformed stage of my life, and in some way they made me question the world I supposedly belonged to. They opened doors for me into another world. When I left the country at the age of eleven, I grieved most over losing them. A thousand years later, I came upon the novels of the Indian writer R. K. Narayan in a London bookstore. I bought every one and imagined they were by my never forgotten friend Narayan. I saw his face behind the sentences, imagined his tall body sitting at a humble desk by his small bedroom window, knocking off a chapter about Malgudi before being called by my aunt to do something or other. '*The streets would be quite dark when I set out to the river for my ablutions, except for the municipal lamps which flickered (if they had not run out of oil) here and there in our street . . . All along the way I had my well-defined encounters. The milkman, starting on his rounds, driving ahead of him a puny white cow, greeted me respectfully and asked, "What is the time, master?" – a question I allowed to die without a reply as I carried no watch . . . The watchman at the Taluk office called from beneath his rug, "Is that you?" – the only question which deserved a reply. "Yes, it's me," I always said and passed on.*'

I knew my friend had perceived such details on our morning walks along the High Level Road. I knew the bullock cart driver, I knew the asthmatic who ran the cigarette stall.

*

AND THEN, ONE DAY, I SMELLED BURNING HEMP ON the ship. For a moment I stood still, then moved towards a staircase where it was stronger, hesitated about whether to go down or up, then climbed the stairs. The smell was coming from a corridor on D level. I stopped where it seemed strongest, got on my knees, and sniffed at the inch of crack under the metal door. I knocked quietly.

'Yes?'

61

I went in.

Sitting at a desk was a gentle-looking man. The room had a porthole. It was open, and the smoke from a rope whose end was burning seemed to follow a path over the man's shoulder and out the porthole. 'Yes?' he asked again.

'I like the smell. I miss it.'

He smiled at me and gestured to a space on his bed where I could sit. He pulled open a drawer and brought out a coil of rope a yard long. It was the same sort of hemp rope that hung slowly burning outside the cigarette stalls in Bambalapitiya or the Pettah market, anywhere in the city, really, where you lit the single smoke you had just bought there; or, if you were running and wanted to cause a disturbance, you used the end of the burning coil to light the fuse of a firecracker.

'I know I shall miss it too,' he said. 'And other things. *Kothamalli*. Balsam. I have such things in my suitcase. For I am leaving forever.' He looked away for a moment. It was as if he had said it aloud to himself for the first time.

'What is your name?'

'Michael,' I said.

'If you are lonely, Michael, you can always come here.'

I nodded, then slipped out and closed the door behind me.

His name was Mr Fonseka and he was travelling to England to be a teacher. I would visit him every few days. He knew passages from all kinds of books he could recite by heart, and he sat at his desk all day wondering about them, thinking what he could say about them. I knew scarcely a thing about the world of literature, but he welcomed me with unusual and interesting stories, stopping abruptly in mid-tale and saying that someday I should find out what happened after that. 'You will like it, I think. Perhaps he will find the eagle.' Or, 'They will escape the maze with the help of someone they are about to meet . . .' Often, during the night, while stalking the adult world with Ramadhin and Cassius, I'd attempt to add to the bare bones of an adventure Mr Fonseka had left unfinished.

He was gracious, with his quietness. When he spoke, he was tentative and languid. Even then I understood his rareness by the pace of his gestures. He stood up only when it was essential, as if he were a sick cat. He was not used to public effort, even though he was now going to be a part of a public world as a teacher of literature and history in England.

I tried to coax him up on deck a few times, but his porthole and what he could see through it seemed enough nature for him. With his books, his burning rope, some bottled Kelani River water, as well as a few family photographs, he had no need to leave his time capsule. I would visit that smoky room if the day was dull, and he would at some point begin reading to me. It was the anonymity of the stories and the poems that went deepest into me. And the curl of a rhyme was something new. I had not thought to believe he was actually quoting something written with care, in some far country, centuries earlier. He had lived in Colombo all his life, and his manner and accent were a product of the island, but at the same time he had this wide-ranging knowledge of books. He'd sing a song from the Azores or recite lines from an Irish play.

I brought Cassius and Ramadhin to meet him. He had

become curious about them, and he made me tell him of our adventures on the ship. He beguiled them as well, especially Ramadhin. Mr Fonseka seemed to draw forth an assurance or a calming quality from the books he read. He'd gaze into an unimaginable distance (one could almost see the dates flying off the calendar) and quote lines written in stone or papyrus. I suppose he remembered these things to clarify his own opinion, like a man buttoning up his own sweater to give warmth just to himself. Mr Fonseka would not be a wealthy man. And it would be a spare life he would be certain to lead as a schoolteacher in some urban location. But he had a serenity that came with the choice of the life he wanted to live. And this serenity and certainty I have seen only among those who have the armour of books close by.

I am aware of the pathos and the irony that come with such a portrait. All those foxed Penguin editions of Orwell and Gissing and the translations of Lucretius with their purple borders that he was bringing with him. He must have believed it would be a humble but good life for an Asian living in England, where something like his Latin grammar could be a distinguishing sword.

I wonder what happened to him. Every few years, whenever I remember, I will look up any reference to Fonseka in a library. I do know that Ramadhin kept in touch with him during his early years in England. But I did not. Though I did realise that people like Mr Fonseka came before us like innocent knights in a more dangerous time, and on the very same path we ourselves were taking now, and at every step there were no doubt the same lessons, *not* poems, to learn brutally by heart, just as there was the discovery of the good and cheap Indian restaurant in Lewisham, and the similar opening up and sealing of blue aerogrammes to Ceylon and later to Sri Lanka, and the same slights and insults and embarrassments over the pronouncing of the letter *v* and our rushed manner of speaking, and most of all the difficulty of *entrance*, and then perhaps a modest acceptance and ease in some similar cabinlike flat.

I think about Mr Fonseka at those English schools wearing his buttoned sweater to protect himself from English weather, and wonder how long he stayed there, and if he did really stay 'forever'. Or whether in the end he could no longer survive it, even though for him it was 'the centre of culture', and instead returned home on an Air Lanka flight that took only two-thirds of a day, to begin again, teaching in a place like Nugegoda. *London returned.* Were all those memorised paragraphs and stanzas of the European canon he brought back the equivalent of a coil of hemp or a bottle of river water? Did he adapt them or translate them, insist on teaching them in a village school, on a blackboard in the sunlight, the rough call of forest birds screeching nearby? Some idea of order at Nugegoda?

WE WERE BY NOW FULLY KNOWLEDGEABLE ABOUT MOST locations on the ship – from the path air ducts took in their journey away from the turbine propellers, to how I could slip into the fish preparation room (by crawling through a trolley exit), because I liked to watch the fish butchers work. Once I balanced with Cassius on the narrow struts above the false ceiling of the ballroom in order to look down at the dancing humans. It was midnight. In six hours, according to our schedules, dead poultry would be carried from the 'cold room' to the kitchens.

We had discovered the door to the armoury had a buggered latch, and when the room was empty we strolled through it, handling the revolvers and handcuffs. And we knew each lifeboat contained a compass, a sail, a rubber raft, plus emergency chocolate bars that we had already eaten. Mr Daniels had finally told us where the poisonous plants were in the fenced section of his garden. He pointed out to us the *Piper mephisticum* that 'sharpened the mind'. He said elders in the Pacific Islands always took it before a critical peace treaty was debated. And there was the curare, growing almost secretly by itself under an intense yellow light, which when inserted into the bloodstream, he told us, was able to knock out the recipient into a long, unremembered trance.

We were also aware of more informal timetables, ranging from when the Australian began her roller-skating, before dawn, to the late hour, when we waited at the lifeboat for the prisoner to appear. We studied him carefully. We could see that round each of his wrists was a metal cuff. These were connected by a chain about eighteen inches long, so his hands were allowed some movement, and there was a padlock.

We watched him in silence. There was no communication between him and the three of us. Save one night, when all at once he paused in his walk and glared into the darkness towards us. He could not see us. But it was as if he was conscious of us there, that he had picked up our scent. The guards did not notice us, only he did. He gave a loud growl and turned away. We must have been fifteen yards away, and he was manacled, but he terrified us.

A Spell

IF OUR JOURNEY TO ENGLAND WAS RECORDED FOR ANY reason in the newspapers of the time, it was because of the presence on the *Oronsay* of the philanthropist Sir Hector de Silva. He had boarded the ship and was travelling with a retinue that included two doctors, one ayurvedic, a lawyer, and his wife and daughter. Most of them stayed in the upper echelons of the ocean liner and were seldom seen by us. No one in his party accepted the invitation to eat at the Captain's Table. It was assumed they were above even that. Although the reason was that Sir Hector, a Moratuwa entrepreneur, who had ground out his fortune in gems, rubber and plots of land, was now suffering from a possibly fatal illness and was on his way to Europe to find a doctor who would save him.

Not one English specialist had been willing to come to Colombo to deal with Sir Hector's medical problem, in spite of being offered considerable remuneration. Harley Street would remain in Harley Street, in spite of a recommendation from the British governor, who had dined with Sir Hector in his Colombo mansion, and in spite of the fact that Sir Hector had been knighted in England for his donations to various charities. So now he was cocooned in a grand double suite on the *Oronsay*, suffering from hydrophobia. At first we did not concern ourselves with Sir Hector's illness. His presence on board ship was seldom mentioned by those at the Cat's Table. He was famous because of his great wealth, and that did not hold any interest for us. But what did make us curious was our discovery of the background to his fateful journey.

It had happened this way. One morning Hector de Silva had been breakfasting on his balcony with friends. They were joking among themselves in the way that those whose lives are safe and comfortable entertain one another. At that moment, a venerable *battaramulle* – or holy priest – walked past the house. Seeing the monk, Sir Hector punned off the title by saying, 'Ah, there goes a *muttaraballa.*' *Muttara* means 'urinating', and *balla* means 'dog'. Therefore, 'There goes a urinating dog.'

It was a quick-witted but inappropriate remark. Having overheard the insult, the monk paused, pointed to Sir Hector, and said, 'I'll send *you* a *muttaraballa . . .*' After which the venerable, reputedly a practitioner of witchcraft, went straight to the temple, where he chanted several mantras, thereby sealing the fate of Sir Hector de Silva and closing the door on his affluent life.

I cannot remember who told us the first part of that story, but the curiosity among Cassius and Ramadhin and me immediately pulled the millionaire's presence in Emperor Class into the foreground of our thoughts. We were busy trying to find out as much as we possibly could after that. I even sent a note to my supposed guardian Flavia Prins, and she met me briefly by the entrance to First Class and said she knew nothing. She was annoyed because my note had hinted at an emergency and I had interrupted one of her important bridge games. The problem was that at the Cat's Table, the others were not talking about it much. Not enough for us. So we eventually approached the Assistant Purser (who, Ramadhin noted, had a glass eye), and he was able to reveal more.

Sometime after the episode with the passing venerable, Sir Hector was coming down the stairs of his great house. (The Assistant Purser used the phrase 'climbing down the staircase'.) His pet terrier was at the foot of the steps waiting to greet him. A usual occurrence. This was an animal loved by all members of the family. As Sir Hector bent down, the affectionate animal leapt for his neck. Sir Hector pulled the dog off, at which point the animal bit his hand.

Two servants eventually got hold of the creature and put it in a kennel. While the animal was being caged, an in-law treated the bite. Apparently the terrier had already behaved strangely that morning, racing around the kitchen under the feet of the servants, and had been chased out of the house with a broom, before slipping back calm and muted at the last minute so it could await its master at the foot of the stairs. The dog had bitten no one during the earlier fracas.

Later that day Sir Hector passed the kennel and wagged his bandaged finger at the animal. Twenty-four hours later the dog died, having shown symptoms of rabies. But by then the 'urinating dog' had already delivered his message.

One by one they came. Every respected doctor who serviced Colombo 7 was brought in for consultation for a cure. Sir Hector was (save for a few illegal gunrunners or gem merchants whose worth would always be unknown) the richest man in the city. The doctors spoke in whispers all the way down the long corridors of his house, arguing and finessing the defence against rabies, which was already beginning to affect the wealthy body upstairs. The virus was travelling at five to ten millimetres per hour to other cells, and there were already symptoms, such as burning, itching and numbness at the site of the bite, but the terrible signs of hydrophobia were not yet apparent. As the patient was being given supportive care, the duration of the illness might last as long as twenty-five days before it was fatal. The terrier was dug up and checked once more to be certain of rabies. Telegrams were sent to Brussels, Paris and London. And three staterooms were booked on the *Oronsay*, which was the next ship leaving for Europe, just in case. The liner would stop at Aden, Port Said and Gibraltar, and it was hoped a specialist would be able to meet with the vessel in at least one of these locations.

But it was also being said that Sir Hector should remain at home, as it was likely that his condition would worsen during a possibly rough voyage where medical facilities might be minimal; plus the fact that there was usually a second-rate doctor on board, usually some twenty-eight-year-old intern whose parents had pull at the Orient Line headquarters. Besides, ayurvedic practitioners were now also arriving at the house from the Moratuwa district, where the de Silva family *walauwa* had existed for more than a century, and these men claimed to have successfully treated victims of rabies. They argued that Sir Hector, by remaining on the island, would be close to the country's most powerful herbal remedies. They spoke vociferously in the old dialects he was familiar with from his youth, saying that the journey would leave him far from these potent sources. As the cause of the illness was local, the antidote would always be found somewhere in the same place.

In the end, Sir Hector decided to take the ship to England. Acquiring wealth he had also acquired a complete faith in the advancements of Europe. Perhaps this would prove to be his fatal flaw. The ship's journey was twenty-one days long. He assumed he would be driven instantly from the Tilbury docks to the best doctor in Harley Street, where, he thought, perhaps there would be a respectful crowd outside, with maybe a few Ceylonese who were fully aware of his financial status. Hector de Silva had read one Russian novel and he could imagine it all, whereas a cure in Colombo seemed to rely on village magic, astrology, and botanical charts in a spidery handwriting. He had grown up knowing some local cures, such as quickly urinating on a foot to alleviate the pain from sea pencils. Now he was being told that for a mad dog's bite the seeds of the black *ummattaka*, or thorn apple, should be soaked in cow piss, ground into a paste, and taken internally. Then, twenty-four hours later, he should take a cold bath and drink buttermilk. The provinces were full of these cures. Four out of ten of them worked. That wasn't good enough.

However, Sir Hector de Silva did coerce one Moratuwa ayurvedic to accompany him on the sea voyage and to bring his sack full of locally gathered herbs and some Nepal-grown *ummattaka* seeds and roots. Thus, along with two established doctors, this ayurvedic boarded the ship. These medical men shared a suite on one side of Sir Hector's central bedroom, while his wife and his twenty-three-year-old daughter shared one on the other side.

And so in mid-ocean the Moratuwa ayurvedic opened up his steamer trunk, which contained unguents and fluids, brought out the thorn apple seeds that he had previously immersed in cow's urine, mixed them with some jaggery paste to disguise the flavour, and scurried down the hall to give the millionaire a cup of this catarrh-like sauce to swallow, followed by a good French brandy, which the philanthropist insisted on. This was carried out twice a day, and it was the ayurvedic's only duty. So while the two professional doctors looked after the patient for the rest of the day, the man from Moratuwa had the run of the ship, though it was made clear his strolls were limited to Tourist Class. He too must have wandered about the vessel, aware of the lack of smells on the obsessively cleansed ship, until one day he picked up the familiar perfume of burning hemp and followed it to its source on D level, paused at the metal door, knocked, heard a response, and entered to be welcomed by Mr Fonseka and a boy.

We had been at sea several days when this visit occurred. And it would be the ayurvedic who revealed the last few details of the Hector de Silva story, with hesitation at first, but eventually nearly every interesting detail came from him. Later on, through us, he met Mr Daniels, who befriended him and invited him down to the hold to view his garden, where they spent hours arguing and discussing the forensics of plants. Cassius too made a new friend of the ayurvedic and immediately requested a few betel leaves from the southern doctor, who had brought a cache with him.

The surreal revelations about the man with a curse on his head thrilled us. We gathered every fragment of Sir Hector's story and remained hungry for more. We cast our minds back to the night of embarkation in Colombo harbour and tried to recall, or to imagine at least, a stretcher, and the body of the millionaire being carried at a slight tilt up the gangplank. Whether we had witnessed this or not, the scene was now indelible in our minds. For the first time in our lives we were interested in the fate of the upper classes; and gradually it became clear to us that Mr Mazappa and his musical legends and Mr Fonseka with his songs from the Azores and Mr Daniels with his plants, who had been until then like gods to us, were only minor characters, there to watch how those with real power progressed or failed in the world.

Afternoons

IT HAD BEEN EVIDENT WHEN MR DANIELS OFFERED THE three of us betel leaves to chew that Cassius was already familiar with them. By the time he was told he would be going to a school in England, he could already aim a jet of the red fluid through his teeth and hit anything he wished – a face on a billboard, the trousers that covered a teacher's buttocks, a dog's head through the open window of a passing car. Preparing for his departure, his parents, hoping to cure this street habit, refused to let him pack any betel leaves, but Cassius stuffed his favourite pillowcase with a mother lode of leaves and nuts. During the emotional farewell in Colombo harbour, as his parents waved to him from the jetty, Cassius pulled out one green leaf and waved it back at them. He was never sure if they saw it, but he hoped they had witnessed his guile.

We had been banned from the Lido pool for three days. Our assault on it that afternoon, armed with deckchairs, and under the influence of Mr Daniels's 'white beedi', meant that all we could do was skulk the perimeter, pretending we were about to leap in. In our turbine room headquarters we decided to find out all we could about the passengers at the Cat's Table, sharing any information we had picked up on our own. Cassius reported that Miss Lasqueti, the wan-looking woman who sat next to him at meals, had accidentally or intentionally 'jostled his penis' with her elbow. I said that Mr Mazappa, who as Sunny Meadows wore black-rimmed spectacles, did so to appear more reliable and thoughtful. He'd plucked them from his breast pocket and passed them over to me to show they were just clear glass. We all felt Mr Mazappa's past must have been a furtive one. 'As the good book says, I have crawled up a few sewers in my time,' was one of his favourite conclusions to an anecdote.

During one of our constant palavers in the turbine room, Cassius said, 'Remember the bogs at St Thomas' College?' He was lying back against a life preserver sucking condensed milk out of a tin. 'You know what I am going to do, before I get off this ship? I promise you I am going to take a shit in the Captain's enamel toilet.'

I spent more time with Mr Nevil again. With those blueprints of the ship that he always carried, he located for me where the engineers ate and slept, and where the Captain's quarters were. He showed me how the electrical system worked its way into every room, and even the way unseen machines spread themselves throughout the lower levels of the *Oronsay*. I was already aware of that. In my cabin, one extended limb of a driveshaft revolved behind a panelled wall continuously, and I often put my open palm against the permanently warm wood.

Best of all, he told me about his days as a ship dismantler, and how an ocean liner could be broken down into thousands of unrecognisable pieces in a 'breaker's yard'. I realised this was what I must have seen in that far corner of Colombo harbour when the ship was being burned. It was being reduced to just useful metal, so the hull could be converted into a canal barge or the funnel hammered out to waterproof a tank. The far corner of all harbours, Mr Nevil said, was where such destructions took place. Alloys were separated, wood burned away, rubber and plastic melted into slabs and buried. But porcelain, metal taps and electrical wiring were saved and reused, so I imagined those who worked with him must have ranged from muscular men who dismantled walls with heavy wooden mallets to those whose specific job it was to pluck and gather coils of metal and small electrical fixtures and door locks, like crows. In a month they could make a ship disappear, leaving only its skeleton in the muck of some estuary, bones for a dog. Mr Nevil had worked all over the world doing this, from Bangkok to Barking. Now he was sitting with me, remembering the harbours he had inhabited at one time or another, rolling a piece of blue chalk in his fingers, suddenly meditative.

It was, he murmured, a dangerous profession, of course. And it was painful to realise that nothing was permanent, not even an ocean liner. 'Not even the trireme!' he said, and nudged me. He had been there to help dismantle the *Normandie* – 'the most beautiful ship ever built' – as it lay charred and half drowned in the Hudson River in America. 'But somehow even *that* was beautiful . . . because in a breaker's yard you discover anything can have a new life, be reborn as part of a car or railway carriage, or a shovel blade. You take that older life and you link it to a stranger.'

Miss Lasqueti

MISS LASQUETI WAS REGARDED BY MOST OF THOSE AT the Cat's Table as a likely spinster, and by us three as having a possible libido (that elbow against Cassius's scrotum). She was lithe, and white as a pigeon. She was not fond of the sun. You would see her in a deckchair reading crime novels within the rectangles of deep shadow, her bright blonde hair a little sparkle in her chosen gloom. She was a smoker. She and Mr Mazappa would simultaneously rise and excuse themselves after the first course and take the nearest exit onto the deck. What they spoke of there, we had no idea. They seemed an unlikely pair. Although she had a laugh that hinted it had rolled around once or twice in mud. It surprised you because it emerged from that modest and slim frame; we heard it usually in response to one of Mr Mazappa's ribald stories. She could be whimsical. 'Why is it when I hear the phrase *"trompe l'oeil"* I think of oysters?' I overheard her say once.

Still, most of the time we had barely a fishhook's evidence about Miss Lasqueti's background or career. We considered ourselves good at vacuuming up clues as we coursed over the ship each day, but our certainty about what we discovered grew slowly. We'd overhear something at lunch, or witness a thrown glance or the shake of a head. 'Spanish is a loving tongue – is it not, Mr Mazappa?' Miss Lasqueti had commented, and he had winked back at her from across the table. We were learning about adults simply by being in their midst. We felt patterns emerging, and for a while everything was based on that wink by Mr Mazappa.

A peculiarity of Miss Lasqueti was that she was a sleeper. Someone who at certain hours during the day could barely stay awake. You saw her fighting it. This struggle made her endearing, as if she were forever warding off an unjustified punishment. You'd walk past her in a deckchair, her head falling slowly towards the book she was attempting to read. She was in many ways our table's ghost, for it was also revealed that she sleepwalked, a dangerous habit on a ship. A sliver of white, I see her always, against the dark rolling sea.

What was her future? What had been her past? She was the only one from the Cat's Table who was able to force us out of ourselves in order to imagine another's life. I admit it was mostly Ramadhin who coaxed this empathy from Cassius and me. Ramadhin was always the most generous of the three of us. But for the first time in our lives we began to sense there was an unfairness in someone else's life. Miss Lasqueti had, I remember, 'gunpowder tea', which she mixed with a cup of hot water at our table, then poured into a thermos before she left us for the afternoon. You could actually see the flush enter her face as the drink knocked her awake.

Describing her as 'white as a pigeon' was probably influenced by a later discovery about her: it was revealed that Miss Lasqueti had twenty or thirty pigeons caged somewhere on the ship. She was 'accompanying them' to England, but she breasted her cards about her motive for travelling with them. Then I heard, via Flavia Prins, that an unknown passenger in First Class had informed her that Miss Lasqueti had often been seen in the corridors of Whitehall.

In any case, it seemed to us that nearly all at our table, from the silent tailor, Mr Gunesekera, who owned a shop in Kandy, to the entertaining Mr Mazappa, to Miss Lasqueti, might have an interesting reason for their journey, even if it was unspoken or, so far, undiscovered. In spite of this, our table's status on the *Oronsay* continued to be minimal, while those at the Captain's Table were constantly toasting one another's significance. That was a small lesson I learned on the journey. What is interesting and important happens mostly in secret, in places where there is no power. Nothing much of lasting value ever happens at the head table, held together by a familiar rhetoric. Those who already have power continue to glide along the familiar rut they have made for themselves.

The Girl

IF ANYONE APPEARED TO BE THE MOST POWERLESS PERSON on the ship it was the girl named Asuntha, and it was only gradually that we became aware of her. She seemed to own just a faded green dress. It was all she wore, even during the storms. She was deaf, and that made her seem even more frail and alone. Someone at our table wondered how she had managed to pay for her passage. We watched her once, exercising on a trampoline, and when she was in mid-air, with all that silent space around her, we felt we were witnessing a different person. But as soon as she stopped and walked away, you were not conscious of any agility or strength in her. She was pale, even for a Sinhalese girl. And slight.

She was scared of water. If she was walking past the pool we'd taunt her by threatening to shove handfuls at her, until Cassius had a change of heart and stopped our doing it. We glimpsed a little mercy in Cassius then, and noticed he began to watch over her shyly from that point on. Sunil, The Hyderabad Mind from the Jankla Troupe, seemed to be looking after her. He sat beside her at meals, at the table where Emily also sat, and he'd glance over to the Cat's

Table, horrified at the amount of noise being made by our group.

Asuntha had a specific way of listening. She could hear only with her right ear, and then only if someone spoke clearly and directly into it. In this way she would take the tremor of air ·and interpret it into sound, then words. You could not communicate except by coming intimately close. During lifeboat drills a steward took her aside to explain rules and procedures, while the rest of us were told the same information from a loudspeaker. It felt there were barriers all around her.

It was chance and nothing more that Emily was sitting at the same table as the girl. And if Emily was the glittering public beauty, this girl was the reclusive one. Gradually they seemed to become friends, and we began to see an intensity in their conversations – the whispers, the holding of hands. It was Emily as a very different soul, when she was with the deaf girl.

A THIN WASH OF MORNING RAIN ON THE DECKS WAS
perfect. Between Exit B and Exit C was a twenty-yard stretch
unhindered by deckchairs. We raced towards it in our bare
feet and let ourselves go, sliding along the slippery wood till
we crashed into the railing or a door being suddenly opened
by a passenger coming out to check on the weather. Cassius
felled the ancient Professor Raasagoola Chaudharibhoy during
one record-setting projection of his body. The distance could
be improved during deck scrubbing. Once the layer of soap
was down and not yet mopped, we could slide twice the
distance, overturning pails, colliding into sailors. Even
Ramadhin participated. He was discovering that more than
anything he loved the sea wind in his face. He would stand
for hours at the prow, his gaze locked into the distance,
hypnotised by something out there or held in some thought.

If anyone wished to capture the daily movements on our
ship, the most accurate method might be to create a series of
time-lapse criss-crossings, depicted in different colours, to

reflect the daily loitering. There was the path Mr Mazappa took after waking at noon, and the stroll the Moratuwa ayurvedic made when free of his duties with Sir Hector. There were the two dog walkers, Hastie and Invernio; the slow perambulation to and from the Delilah Lounge by Flavia Prins and her bridge-playing friends; the Australian circling on skates at dawn; the Jankla Troupe's official and unofficial activities; as well as the three of us bursting all over the place like freed mercury: stopping at the pool, then the ping-pong table, watching a piano class with Mr Mazappa in the ballroom, a small nap, a chat with the one-eyed Assistant Purser – looking carefully into his glass eye as we passed – and visits to Mr Fonseka's cabin for an hour or more. All these haphazard patterns of movement became as predictable as the steps of a quadrille.

For us, this was an era without the benefit of photography so the journey escaped any permanent memory. Not even one blurred snapshot of my time on the *Oronsay* exists in my possession to tell me what Ramadhin really looked like during that journey. A blurred dive into the swimming pool, a white-sheeted body dropping through the air into the sea, a boy searching for himself in a mirror, Miss Lasqueti asleep in a deckchair – these are images only from memory. On the upper deck, in Emperor Class, some passengers had box cameras, and they were often captured in their 'soup and fish' outfits. At the Cat's Table, Miss Lasqueti now and then did sketches in a yellow notebook. She may have drawn some of us, but we were never curious enough to ask, an artistic interest not being something we assumed in those around us. She could just as easily have been knitting a portrait of each of us using

85

different-coloured wools. We were more curious when she brought out her pigeon jacket to show us how she could walk around on deck carrying several live birds in its padded pockets.

Whatever we did had no possibility of permanence. We were simply discovering how long our lungs could hold air as we raced back and forth along the bottom of the pool. Because our greatest pleasure was when one hundred spoons were flung by a steward into the pool and Cassius and I dived in with competitors to collect as many as we could in our small hands, relying on those lungs for more and more time underwater. We were watched and cheered and laughed at if our trunks slipped down as we clambered out like amphibious fish with cutlery in our hands, gripping them against our chests. 'I love all men who dive,' Melville, that great sea-crosser, wrote. And if I had been asked to choose a career then, or at any time during those twenty-one days, I would have said I desired to be a diver in some similar competition for the rest of my life. It never occurred to me then that there was no such trade or profession. Still our slim bodies, almost part of the element, dumped our treasure and flipped back in for another helping, hunting underwater for the last spoons. Only Ramadhin, protecting his tentative heart, could not participate. But he would, slightly bored, cheer us on.

Thievery

ONE MORNING I WAS PERSUADED BY A MAN KNOWN TO us as Baron C. to help with a project. He needed a small, athletic boy, and he had been watching me dive for spoons in the pool.

First of all I was invited by him to have some ice cream in the First Class lounge. Then, in his cabin, in order to demonstrate my skill, I was asked to remove my sandals, get on the furniture, and move as fast as I could around the room, without ever touching the floor. I thought this was peculiar, but I leapt from the armchair onto the desk, then to the bed, and swung myself hanging on the door over to the bathroom. Compared with mine it was a very large cabin, and after a few minutes I stood there, barefoot on the thick carpet, panting like a dog. At which point he brought out a pot of tea.

'It's Colombo tea, not ship tea,' he said, adding condensed milk into the cup. The man knew what good tea was. So far, we had been served what tasted like dishwater on the ship, and I had stopped drinking it. In fact, I would not drink tea for years. But the Baron made me my last good cup of tea. He had brought out very small cups, so I had to have several that day.

The Baron told me I was *athletic*. He walked me to his door and pointed to the window above it. It was rectangular and had a small latch that could secure it shut. Now the glass lay horizontal, flat like a tray, allowing the air to come into and go out of the room.

'Think you can climb through that?' Not waiting for an answer, he cupped his hands and made me climb onto them and up onto his shoulders. I was six feet from the ground. I began crawling into the opening, precarious on the glass and its wooden frame, scared I would fall through. Protecting this open space further were two horizontal bars. He asked me to try working my body between them, but I could not get through.

'It is no use. Get down.' I put my knees on his shoulders again and held on to his brilliantined hair and climbed down, feeling I had betrayed him in some way, especially after the ice cream and the good tea.

'I'll have to try someone else,' he murmured to himself, as if I were no longer in his presence. And then, conscious of my disappointment, he said, 'I am sorry.'

The next day I saw the Baron at the pool speaking with another boy, who a short while later accompanied him to the upper deck. He was smaller than I was, though perhaps not as *athletic*, because the boy returned within an hour and talked only about the tea and biscuits he had been given. Then, perhaps a day after that, I was invited by the Baron to come to his cabin and attempt to climb through that window again. He had, he said, another idea. As we passed the steward who guarded the entrance to First Class, the Baron said, 'My nephew

– having him over for tea.' And soon I was strolling legally through the carpeted lounge, keeping my eyes open for Flavia Prins, for this was also her territory.

He had asked me to wear my swimsuit, and when I removed the rest of my clothes he brought out a small pail of motor oil that he'd managed to get from the engine room, and made me spread the thick black liquid all over my body from the neck down. Then once again I was hoisted up to the open window, beyond which were the two horizontal bars. And this time, covered in oil, I slid through like an eel and dropped to the floor of the corridor on the other side of the door. I knocked and he let me back in. He was grinning.

Immediately he gave me a bathrobe to wear and we went along the empty corridor. He knocked at a door, and when there was no response he hoisted me up with his palms, and this time I slipped through the open window the other way, *into* a stateroom. I unlocked the door from inside, and as the Baron entered, he patted me on the head. He sat in an armchair briefly, winked at me, then got up and began looking around the room, opening up a few cupboard drawers. We were out in minutes.

Looking back, I think he may have convinced me that the breaking and entering that followed was a private game between him and some friends. For what he was doing seemed relaxed and good-natured. He strolled through a suite, his hands casually in his trouser pockets as he peered at objects on a shelf or a desk, or glanced into further rooms. I recall he once found a large sheaf of papers that he dropped into a sports bag. I also saw him pocket a silver-bladed knife.

While he did this, I was mostly looking out from one of the portholes at the sea. If they were open I'd hear yells from quoits players on a lower deck. That was the excitement for me, and being in such a large cabin. The one I shared with Mr Hastie was about the size of a stateroom's large bed. I walked into one fully mirrored bathroom and suddenly saw receding images of myself, semi-naked, covered in black oil, just a brown face and spiky hair. There was a wild boy in there, somebody from one of the *Jungle Book* stories whose eyes watched me, white as lamps. This was, I think, the first reflection or portrait that I remember of myself. It was the image of my youth that I would hold on to for years – someone startled, half formed, who had not become anyone or anything yet. I became aware of the Baron on the edge of the mirror frame, watching me. He had a considering look. It was as if he understood what I was seeing in the mirror, as if he too had done that once. He threw me a towel and asked me to clean myself up and put on the rest of my clothes, which he'd brought in his sports bag.

I could not wait to tell the others at the next turbine room meeting what had happened to me. I felt my authority grow. But in retrospect I see that what the Baron gave me was another self, something as small as a pencil sharpener. It was a little escape into being somebody else, a door I would postpone opening for some years, at least until I was beyond my teens. Those half-blurred afternoons remain with me. I remember one day, after he had knocked on a door and got no reply and I had slid through the bars of the window frame and let him in, we were shocked to find someone asleep in the large bed, the table beside him arrayed with medicine bottles. The Baron held up his palm for silence, went closer, and stared at the comatose body, which I would realise later was Sir Hector de Silva. The Baron touched my shoulder and gestured to a metal bust of the millionaire on the dresser. While the Baron continued looking around the room for valuables – gems, I supposed; that was, after all, what thieves seemed to take – I looked back and forth, comparing the metal head with the real one. The bust made the sleeping man look leonine and noble, in contrast to the reality that rested on the pillow. I tried lifting the bust into my arms, but it was too heavy.

The Baron now leafed through documents but did not take any. Instead he plucked a small green statue of a frog off the mantelpiece. 'Jade,' he bent down and whispered to me. And then, almost too personally, he took a photograph of a young woman that was in a silver frame beside the man's bed. He told me, as we walked down the corridor a few minutes later, that he found her very attractive. 'Perhaps,' he said, 'I will meet her at some point during this journey.'

The Baron would disembark, prematurely, at Port Said, for by then, suspicions of a thief on board were making the rounds, although they were not of course directed at anyone in First Class. I know that at Aden he mailed off some packages. In any case, all of a sudden he stopped asking me to meet him. He took me for a final tea in the Bedford Lounge, and I hardly saw him from then on. I never knew whether he had been stealing simply to cover his First Class passage or to give money to an ailing brother or some old partner in crime. He seemed to me a generous man. I still remember how he looked, how he dressed, although I am not sure if he was English or one of those mongrels who have assumed the panache of aristocracy. I do know that whenever I am in a country where they put up the faces of criminals in post offices, I look for him.

OUR SHIP CONTINUED TO MOVE NORTH-WEST, CROSSING into higher latitudes, and the passengers could feel the nights becoming cooler. One day we were told over the loudspeakers that a film would be shown after the dinner sitting, on the deck outside the Celtic Room. By dusk stewards had set up a stiff sheet at the stern and brought out a projector, which they covered mysteriously. Half an hour before the film began, about a hundred people had made up a restless audience, the adults sitting on chairs, the children on the deck itself. Ramadhin and Cassius and I got as close to the screen as possible. This was our first film. There was a loud crackling in the speakers, and suddenly images were thrown onto the screen, which was surrounded by a receding purple sky.

We were just days away from landing in Aden, so the choice of *The Four Feathers* was, I see now, somewhat tactless, as it attempted to compare the brutality of Arabia with a civilised though foolish England. We watched an Englishman having his face branded (we got to hear the sizzle of his flesh) so that he could pass himself off as an Arab in an invented desert nation. An old general in the story referred to the Arabs as something like *'the Gazarra tribe – irresponsible and violent'*. Later another Englishman was blinded by staring at the desert sun, and he wandered slowly about for the rest of the film. As for the subtler issues of jingoism and cowardice in a time of war, those were blown away by the strong winds into the passing ocean. The sound system was not good, besides which we were not used to atonal English accents. We simply followed the action. There was also the possibility of an additional subplot: for our ship was approaching a storm zone, and if we turned our heads away from the drama on the screen we could see forks of lightning in the distance.

The movie, as we rolled under the gradually disappearing stars, was being shown in two locations. It had begun half an hour earlier in the Pipe and Drums Bar in First Class, projected to a quieter group of about forty well-dressed passengers; when the first reel was over, that segment of the film was rewound and carried in a metal container down to our projector on deck for its alfresco showing, while the First Class audience watched the second reel. As a result, there were confusing fall-outs of sound that merged the two screenings. The volume on every speaker was turned to maximum because of the roar of the sea winds, and we were constantly assaulted by contrapuntal noises; while watching a tense scene we could hear rousing songs in an officers' mess. Still, our alfresco showing had the atmosphere of a night picnic. We were all given a cup of ice cream, and as we waited for the First Class reel to be over and then threaded onto our projector, the Jankla Troupe performed. They were doing a juggling act with large butcher knives just at the moment we heard the bloodthirsty screaming of attacking

Arabs from the speakers in First Class. The Jankla Troupe was parodying these yells with comic body movements, and then The Hyderabad Mind stepped forward to announce that a brooch someone had lost the day before could be found hanging over the projector's lens. And so, just as First Class was witnessing the brutal massacre of English troops, exultant cheers rose from our audience.

Our film proceeded on the seemingly live canvas of a flapping screen. The plot was full of grandness and confusion, of acts of cruelty that we understood and responsible honour that we did not. Cassius would go around for days claiming to be part of 'the Oronsay tribe – irresponsible and wiolent.'

Unfortunately, the anticipated storm burst loose over the ship, and as the rain hit the projector the hot metal began hissing. A steward attempted to hold an umbrella over it. A gust ripped the screen loose and sent it skittering over the ocean like a ghost, and the images continued to be shot out, targetless, over the sea. We never learned the end of the story, not on that journey. I did a few years later, by reading A. E. W. Mason's novel in the Dulwich College library. He turned out to be an old boy of the school. In any case, that night saw the beginning of violent storms that assaulted the *Oronsay*. It was only after this was over that we escaped the turmoil of the ocean and landed in the real Arabia.

THERE ARE TIMES WHEN A STORM INVADES THE landscape of the Canadian Shield, where I live during the summers, and I wake up believing I am in mid-air, at the height of the tall pines above the river, watching the approaching lightning, and hearing behind it the arrival of its thunder. It is only from such a height that you see the great choreography and danger of storms. In the house, a few bodies are asleep, and near them the hound, her ears tormented, shaking, as if her heart is about to collapse or be flung out. I have seen her face in the half-light of such storms as if within the velocity of some space-travel experiment, the normally beautiful features thrust back. And while the others sleep, rocked in this wild nature, only the river below looks stable. During the rips of light, you see the acres of trees capsized, everything tilted in a biblical palm. A few times every summer this happens. I expect and so prepare for the arrival of the thunder with this dog, this sweet hunter.

Of course there is a *why* to all this. For I have been in that hovering unsafe place with no grounding to the unknown miles below. All these years later it returns – the night with Cassius after we had tethered ourselves to the deck of the ship in preparation for what we thought would be an exciting adventure.

Perhaps it had been the failure of that film to satisfy us. I still cannot explain why we did what we then did. It may simply have been because it was to be our first sighting of a storm at sea. After the projector had been rolled away and the chairs stacked, there was a sudden lull upon the ocean and in the sky above us. So that now, even though we were told that the radar had blinked the existence of another approaching upheaval, the winds had quieted, and this gave us time to prepare ourselves.

It was Cassius, of course, who persuaded me into the best seat in the house for the catastrophe. We talked it over near the lifeboats. Ramadhin did not wish to participate, but he offered to help set it up. A day earlier we had come across some ropes and tackle in a storeroom that had been left open during the lifeboat drill. And so, that night during the lull, while nearly all the other passengers had returned to their cabins, we made our way to the open Promenade Deck, near the bow, and found various permanent objects we could attach ourselves to with the ropes. We heard the Captain announce that they were expecting a fifty-knot gale and to prepare for the worst.

Cassius and I lay on our backs, side by side, and Ramadhin began to tie us with ropes to some V-shaped rivets and a bollard. He was hurrying, for he could see the storm coming.

He checked his knots in the darkness and left us there, spread-eagled and tightly harnessed. The deck was deserted, and not much happened for a while, save for a light rain. Perhaps we had veered away from the storm. But then the gale hit and pulled the air out of our mouths. We had to turn our heads away from its rush in order to breathe, the wind buckling like metal around us. We'd imagined lying there conversing in wonder about the lights of the storm at some great height above us, but we were now almost drowning from the water in the air – the rain, and the sea that was leaping over the railings and swirling across the deck. Lightning lit the rain in the air above us, and then it was dark once more. A loose rope was slapping at my throat. There was only noise. We could not tell if we were screaming or only trying to.

With each wave it sounded as if the ship was breaking apart, and with each wave the wash covered us until we were tilted upright again. We were aware of a constant rhythm. Whenever the ship ploughed into the oncoming sea, we were swept around within the surf, unbreathing, while the stern rose into the air, the propellers out of their element screaming till they fell back down into the sea, and we on the bow leapt up again, unnaturally.

As I lay on the Promenade Deck of the *Oronsay*, during those few hours when we believed we had given up any chance of our lives, everything coalesced. I was something orderless in a jar, unable to escape what was happening, unable to get out of what was occurring. All I held on to was that I was not alone. Cassius was with me. Now and then our heads turned simultaneously in the lightning and we each saw the blunt, washed-out face of the other. I felt I was caught in this place. If and when the ship pivoted its nose down and descended, overcome by some towering wave, Cassius and I would still be permanently tied to a pump generator or some such thing. There was no one else. We were the only ones on the surface of the ship, as if staked out for sacrifice.

The waves shattered, rolled over us, and disappeared overboard as quick as a nightmare. Then we rose. Then we dropped into the next valley. All that was holding us to safety was Ramadhin's slight knowledge of knots. What did he know of knots? We assumed in our death throes that he had no knowledge of them. We were not safe at all. There was no sense of time. How long were we there before we were blinded by searchlights focused down from the bridge onto the two of us? Even in our frayed state we sensed the outrage behind the light. Then it went out.

Later we learned all the names for storms. *Chubasco. Squall. Cyclone. Typhoon.* And later we were told what it was like below deck, how the stained-glass windows in the Caledonia Room shattered and the electrical circuits burned out almost at once, so there were flashlights moving up and down the hallways, swaying their beams into the bars and lounges as people searched for missing passengers. Lifeboats broke partially free of their davits and hung tilted in mid-air. The ship's compasses spun. Mr Hastie and Mr Invernio were in the lightless kennels attempting to calm the dogs tormented by the thunder in their ears. One wave hit the Assistant Purser, and the force of it washed out his glass eye. All this while our heads were stretched back to try to see how deep the bow would go on its next descent. Our screams unheard, even to each other, even to ourselves, even if the next day our throats were raw from yelling into that hallway of the sea.

It seemed like hours before someone nudged me. The storm was still active but calm enough now to send three sailors out to our rescue. They cut the ropes, the swelling knots had fused, and we were carried down a flight of stairs to a dining cabin that was doubling as a medical centre. There had been a few bashes to the head and broken fingers during the last hour or two. We were stripped down and each given a blanket. We were told we could sleep there. I recall that when I was lifted by the sailor, there was such warmth in his body. I remember that when someone removed my shirt he said that all of the buttons had been knocked loose.

I saw Cassius's face as if all intricacy had been washed away. Then, just before we fell asleep, Cassius leaned over and whispered, *'Don't forget. Someone did this to us.'*

A few hours later three officers were sitting across from us. We had been woken and I was now expecting the worst. We would be sent back to Colombo, perhaps, or beaten. But as soon as the officers sat down, Cassius said, 'Someone did this to us, I don't know who . . . They were masked,' he added.

This startling revelation meant the interrogation by the officers would take much longer, in order for us to convince them this was the truth, though the burn marks from the ropes partly told them we could not have done this to ourselves. They offered us some ship tea, and we thought we had got away with our story, when a steward came in and said the Captain wished to see us. Cassius winked at me. He had often spoken of wanting to see the Captain's cabin.

One of the officers, we discovered later, had already gone down to Ramadhin's cabin, because of his known connection to us. Ramadhin had pretended sleep and when woken pretended a lack of knowledge once he was told we were alive and had not been washed overboard. That must have been around midnight. Now it was two in the morning. We were given bathrobes and marched into the presence of the Captain. Cassius was looking around the room, regarding the furnishings, when the Captain's hand slammed down on his desk.

We had seen the Captain only look bored or smile falsely when making public announcements. Now he erupted with a performance, as if he had just been released from a cage. The reprimands began with a mathematical precision. He pointed out that eight sailors had been involved in our rescue – for more than thirty minutes. This resulted in at least, *at least*, four hours of wasted time, and as the average salary of a sailor was X pounds an hour, X times four was what it had cost the Orient Line, *plus* the Head Steward's time at another Y pounds an hour. Plus double-time payments that were always made during emergencies. Plus the Captain's time, considerably more expensive. 'Our ship therefore will bill your parents for nine hundred pounds!' he said, signing some formal-looking papers that for all I knew could have been his memo to English Customs to keep us out of England. He slammed the table again, threatened that he would put us off at the ship's first landfall, and proceeded to blaggard our ancestors. Cassius attempted to interrupt him with what he thought was a remark of courteous humility.

'Thank you so much for rescuing us, Uncle.'

'Shut up you . . . you' – he was searching – *'viper'.*

'Wiper, sir?'

The Captain paused and watched Cassius to determine if he was mocking him. He must have felt he was at a secure moral height.

'No. You are a polecat. An Asian polecat, a loathsome little Asian polecat. You know what I do when I find a polecat in my house? I set fire to its testicles.'

'I like polecats, sir.'

'You repulsive, wet, snivelling . . .'

In the silence that followed, as he continued searching for insults, the door to the Captain's bathroom swung open and we saw his enamel commode. We were no longer interested in the Captain. Cassius groaned and said, 'Uncle, I feel sick . . . Would it be possible to use your—'

'Get out! You little cunt!'

We were escorted by two sailors to our cabins.

Flavia Prins peered closely at her bracelet as she spoke to me in the slightly damaged Caledonia Room. An abrupt note from her had insisted I meet her promptly. We had by now been processed through various interrogators, and it had been insisted in every case that we never mention what had occurred. Or we would be in more trouble. But we had mentioned it to two of our tablemates during the next morning's breakfast. The

dining room was almost empty, and only Miss Lasqueti and
Mr Daniels were eating with us. When we told them, they did
not seem to think it was that serious. 'Not for you, but damn
serious for them,' Miss Lasqueti said. She was, we would
discover, one for the rule books. Besides, she was more
impressed by Ramadhin's knots, which she said had 'saved
your bacon'. But now, as I approached Flavia Prins, I realised
I might be in trouble with my unofficial guardian. She loosened
and resnapped her bracelet, ignoring me, then struck like a
bird suddenly pecking at the forehead of a dog.

'What happened last night?'

'There was a storm,' I said.

'You thought there was a *storm?*'

I wondered if she was quite unaware of what we had travelled
through.

'There was a terrible storm, Auntie. We were all scared. We
were shaking in our beds.'

She said nothing, so I carried on.

'I had to call a steward. I kept falling out of my bed. I
walked in the hall till I found Mr Peters, and asked him to tie
me to the bed, and also if he could tie Cassius up too. Cassius
had nearly broken his arm when the ship rolled and something
fell on him. He has a bandage.'

She gazed at me, not quite with awe.

'I saw the Captain last night, in the hospital, when I took
Cassius there. He clapped Cassius on the back and called him
a "brave fellow". Then Mr Peters came down with us and tied
us to our beds. He said there was a man and a woman playing
in one of the lifeboats when the storm happened and they hurt

themselves when it crashed down onto the deck. They are all right, but his "this thing" is hurt. He had to go to the surgery also.'

'I know your uncle very well . . .' She paused for tremendous effect. I was wary of this sentence of hers and began to sense she knew more of last night's events than I thought.

'And I knew your mother, slightly. Your uncle is a judge! How *dare* you speak such falsehoods to *me* – who is so concerned about your safety.'

I blurted out, 'They told me not to say anything, to say nothing about Mr Peters. They said Mr Peters is a "rogue sailor", Auntie. They said they will put him off at first landfall. When we asked him to tie us to our bunks for safety, instead, he took us up and tied us to the deck with these ropes, to punish us for . . . interrupting the card game he was having with some drunk men. He said, "This is what we do to disobedient boys who keep interrupting us!" '

She peered at me. I thought I had her for a moment.

'I never, ever, *ever* met . . .'

Not much happened during the next day. An eastbound steamer passed us at dusk one evening, all of its lights on, and it was a fantasy among the three of us to row over to it and return with them to Colombo. The chief engineer ordered the engines to be slowed while the emergency electrical systems were tested, and for a while it seemed we had stalled in what was now the Arabian Sea. The stillness made us feel we were sleepwalking. Cassius and I went out on the becalmed deck. It was only then, in that peacefulness, that I imagined the full nature of the storm. Of being roofless and floorless. What we had witnessed was only what had been above the sea. Now something shook itself free and came into my mind. It was not only the things we could see that had no safety. There was the underneath.

*

Smuggled among the belongings of the ayurvedic from Moratuwa was a cache of datura leaves and seeds from Pakistan. He had purchased the plant for Sir Hector to dispel the recent disruptions on his body, and also to retard the onset of hydrophobia. Datura was to be the most successful potion the millionaire took during his sea journey. The drug had a reputation for being versatile yet unreliable. Supposedly, if you were laughing when its white flower was picked, it resulted in much laughter, or dancing if that was the activity during the gathering. (As a flower it was most fragrant in the evening.) It was good for fevers and tumours. However, as part of its wayward nature, while under its influence a person would also respond to questions with no hesitation and with utter truthfulness. And Hector de Silva was known as a cautiously untruthful man.

The millionaire's wife, Delia, always considered him maddeningly private. Now, days after leaving Colombo on the *Oronsay*, with the administration of the ayurvedic's drug, she had a chance to uncover the man she had married. Every little crumb from his youth came into view. He exposed the terror from his father's whippings that compartmentalised him and eventually made him a brutal financier. He spoke of his secret visits to his brother, Chapman, who had run away from home, taking a neighbouring girl with whom he was in love, who was known to have an extra finger. They had it chopped off in Chilaw and were living a sane and quiet life in Kalutara.

Delia discovered too the way in which her husband had diverted his money into many underground tributaries. Much of this information was being revealed around the time of the cyclone during which Hector de Silva rolled from side to side on his large bed as the vessel bucked and dived. He actually seemed to be enjoying himself, while his wife and the rest of the retinue scurried from his bed to vomit in their adjacent cabins. The datura had snuffed out any concern in him, as well as any side effect of sickness, and any quality of guardedness. If it was an aphrodisiac, it turned him from a lean and distant partner into a benign companion. At first this character change went unnoticed. The whole ship was in the midst of the storm. A small fire had broken out in the engine room when he began telling the truth for the first time in his adult life. And the dangerous weather had brought out the pickpockets, who always thrived in unstable situations where physical help was needed. Added to this, a whole compartment of grain had got wet and burst loose in the hold, altering the very balance of the ship, so emergency crews were down there shovelling it back as carpenters rebuilt the borders. They worked in darkness in the depths of the hold, with only the spray of an oil lamp, doing 'gravedigger's work', as Joseph Conrad called it, waist deep in the grain. Meanwhile Sir Hector was recalling to his little retinue a small, sweet memory of a gliding car he had driven as a boy at a fair in Colombo. He told the story again and again, unwrapping it as if it were new each time, to his wife and daughter and the three uninterested medical aides.

Whatever the fate might have been for our ship, which was now travelling like a coffin in the cyclone, Sir Hector enjoyed a few good days letting free the truth about his wealth, his hidden pleasures, his genuine affection for his wife, while the vessel plunged into the bowels of the sea and then emerged like an encrusted coelacanth, the ocean pouring off its features, so that machinists, thrown against the red-hot engines, burned their arms, and the supposed cream of the cream of the East stumbled against pickpockets in the long corridors, and band members fell off the dais in the midst of 'Blame It on My Youth', as Cassius and I lay spreadeagled on the Promenade Deck, under the rain.

Gradually the decks and the dining rooms repopulated. Miss Lasqueti came up to us with a smile to say the Head Steward had to enter 'all unusual occurrences' into a logbook, so perhaps we would appear in the ship's records. There had also been a series of 'misplacements' on the ship. Croquet sets were missing, wallets had been lost during the storm. Our Captain appeared and told everyone that a gramophone belonging to a Miss Quinn-Cardiff had gone astray and could not be located, so any knowledge of its whereabouts would be appreciated. Cassius, who had recently been down in the hold to watch the engineers fix a section of bilge pipe, claimed the gramophone was being played there, loudly and constantly. The ship's staff countered this trend of losses with an announcement that an earring had been found, somehow, in a lifeboat, and to please identify and claim it at the Purser's Office. No mention was made of the Assistant Purser's glass eye, though the intercom continued to obsessively list the few objects that had been recovered. *'Found: One brooch. One lady's brown felt hat. One journal belonging to Mr Berridge with unusual pictures.'*

The ship's recovery from the storm and the better weather did mean one good thing. The prisoner was once again allowed his evening walk. We waited for him and eventually saw him standing there on the deck, shackled. He drew a huge breath – taking in all the energy that was in the night air around him – and then he released it, his face full of a sublime smile.

Our ship steamed towards Aden.

Landfall

ADEN WAS TO BE THE FIRST PORT OF CALL, AND DURING the day before our arrival there was a flurry of letter writing. It was a tradition to have one's mail stamped in Aden, where it could be sent back to Australia and Ceylon or onward to England. All of us were longing for the sight of land, and as morning broke we lined up along the bow to watch the ancient city approach, mirage-like out of the arc of dusty hills. Aden had been a great harbour as early as the seventh century B.C. and was mentioned in the Old Testament. It was where Cain and Abel were buried, Mr Fonseka said, preparing us for the city he himself had never seen. It had cisterns built out of volcanic rock, a falcon market, an oasis quarter, an aquarium, a section of town given over to sail makers, and stores that contained merchandise from every corner of the globe. It would be our last footstep in the East. After Aden there would be just half a day's sailing before we entered the Red Sea.

The *Oronsay* cut its engines. We were not docked on the quay but in the outer harbour, at Steamer Point. If passengers wished to go ashore, they could be ferried into the city by barges, and these were already waiting beside our vessel. It was nine in the morning, and without the sea breezes that we were accustomed to, the air was heavy and hot.

That morning the Captain had announced the rules about entering the city. Passengers were allowed just six hours of shore leave. Children could go only if accompanied by 'a responsible male adult'. And women were forbidden to go at all. There was the expected outrage at this, especially among Emily and a group of her friends by the pool who wished to disembark and take on the citizens with their beauty. And Miss Lasqueti was annoyed, for she wished to study the local falcons. She had hoped to bring a few of them blindfolded on the ship. Cassius, Ramadhin and I were concerned mostly with finding someone who was *not* a responsible male, who could be easily distracted, to take us along. Mr Fonseka, in spite of his curiosity, had no plans to leave the ship. Then we heard that Mr Daniels was eager to visit the old oasis to study its vegetation, where, he said, every blade of grass was swollen with water, and thick as your finger. He was also interested in something called 'khat' that he had been talking to the ayurvedic about. We offered to help him transport any plants back to the ship, and he agreed, and we went with him down the rope ladders into a barge as quickly as we could.

We were surrounded instantly by a new language. Mr Daniels was busy negotiating a fee with a hackney to transport us to where the great palms were. His authority seemed diminished by the crowd, so we left him there arguing and slipped away. A carpet salesman gestured to us, offered us tea, and we sat with him for a while, laughing whenever he laughed, nodding when he nodded. There was a small dog that he indicated he wished to give us, but we moved on.

We began to argue about what to see. Ramadhin wanted to visit the aquarium that had been built a few decades earlier. It was obviously something Mr Fonseka had told him about. He was sullen about having to see the markets first. In any case we entered the narrow shops that sold seeds and needles, made coffins, and printed maps and pamphlets. Out on the street you could have the shape of your head read, your teeth pulled. A barber cut Cassius's hair and poked a vicious pair of scissors quickly into his nose to clear away the possibility of any further hair in the nostrils of a twelve-year-old.

I was used to the lush chaos of Colombo's Pettah market, that smell of sarong cloth being unfolded and cut (a throat-catching odour), and mangosteens, and rain-soaked paperbacks in a bookstall. Here was a sterner world, with fewer luxuries. There was no overripe fruit in the gutters. There were in fact no gutters. It was a dusty landscape, as if water had not been invented. The only liquid was the cup of dark tea offered to us by the carpet salesman, along with a delicious, permanently remembered almond sweet. Even if this was a harbour city, the air held hardly a particle of dampness. You had to look closely, for what might be buried away in a pocket – a petite vial of oil for a woman's hair, folded within paper, or a chisel wrapped in oilcloth to protect its blade from the dust in the air.

We entered a concrete building at the edge of the sea. Ramadhin led the way through a maze of mostly subterranean tanks. The aquarium appeared deserted except for a number of garden eels from the Red Sea and a few colourless fish swimming in a foot of saltwater. Cassius and I climbed to another level, where there were taxidermic examples of marine life, lying in dust alongside whatever technical equipment was being stored – a hose, a small generator, a hand pump, a dustpan and brush. We gave the whole place five minutes and revisited all the stores we had been into, this time to say goodbye. The barber, who still had no other customers, gave me a head massage, pouring unknown oils into my hair.

We reached the wharf before the deadline. Out of a too-late courtesy we decided to wait for Mr Daniels on the dock, Ramadhin wrapped up in a djellaba, and Cassius and I hugging ourselves in the brisk air coming from over the ocean. The barges rocked in the water, and we tried guessing which vessels were owned by pirates, for we had been told by a steward that piracy was common here. A cupped hand held up pearls. The afternoon's catch of fish, strewn at our feet, more multicoloured than their indoor ancestors, sparkled whenever buckets of water were sloshed over them. The professions along this promontory belonged to the sea, and the merchants whose laughter and bartering surrounded us were the owners of the world. We realised we had seen just a small sliver of the city; we had only glanced through a keyhole into Arabia. We had missed the cisterns and wherever it was that Cain and Abel were buried, but it had been a day of intricate listening, of careful watching, all our conversations made up of gestures. The sky began to darken out at Steamer Point, or Tawahi, as the bargemen called it.

Finally we saw Mr Daniels striding along the wharf. He was carrying a cumbersome plant in his arms, and was accompanied by two weak-looking men in white suits, each holding a miniature palm. He greeted us cheerfully – obviously he had not been too concerned, if at all, by our disappearance. The slight, moustached figures helping him were silent, and as one of them passed me the small palm, he wiped the sweat from his face, and winked, and smiled, and I saw it was Emily in men's clothes. Beside her was a similarly disguised Miss Lasqueti. Cassius took the palm from her and we carried them onto the barge. Ramadhin got in with us and sat hunched over, bundled up in his cloak, during the ten-minute ride to the ship.

Once back on board, the three of us made our way down to Ramadhin's cabin, where he unfolded his djellaba to reveal the carpet salesman's dog again.

We came on deck an hour later. It was already dark, and the lights on the *Oronsay* were brighter than those on land. The ship had still not moved. In the dining room there were loud conversations about the day's adventures. Only Ramadhin and Cassius and I kept silent. We were so excited by our smuggling of the dog onto the boat we knew that if we spoke just one syllable, we'd slide uncontrollably into the whole story. We had spent the past chaotic hour trying to bathe the animal in Ramadhin's narrow shower stall, avoiding the swipe of its claws. It was clear the creature had never met carbolic soap in his life. We'd dried the dog in Ramadhin's bedsheet and left him in the cabin while we went up to eat.

We listened to the stories as we sat at the Cat's Table, with people interrupting one another. The women were silent. And the three of us were silent. Emily passed by our table and bent down to ask me if I had had a good day. I asked her politely what she had done while we had gone ashore, and she said she had spent the day 'carrying things', then winked at me and went off laughing. One of the things we had missed while walking around Aden was the 'Gully Gully man', who had rowed up to the *Oronsay* and performed magic tricks. Apparently his canoe was partially boarded up so he could stand on a sort of stage while he made chickens appear from his clothing. By the end of his act there were over twenty chickens fluttering around him. There were many Gully Gully men, we were told, and with luck there would be another at Port Said.

There was a shudder during dessert as the boat's engines started. We all got up and went out to the railings to watch the departure, our castle slipping away slowly from the thin horizon of lights, back into the great darkness.

WE GUARDED THE DOG THAT NIGHT. HE WAS FEARFUL of our sudden movements, until Ramadhin managed to bring him into his bunk and fall asleep with his arms around him. When the three of us woke the next morning we had already entered the Red Sea, and it was during this passage, on the first day steaming north, that something astonishing happened.

It had always been difficult to penetrate the barrier that separated us from First Class. Two polite and determined stewards either let you through or turned you away. But even they could not stop Ramadhin's small dog. He had leapt out of Cassius's arms and bolted from the cabin. We ran up and down the empty hallways looking for him. Within moments the little fellow must have emerged into the sunlight of B Deck and run beside the railings, raced perhaps into the lower ballroom, up its gilded staircase, and past the two stewards into First Class. They managed to grab him, but soon he was free again. He had eaten none of the food we had offered him, which we'd smuggled out of the dining room in our trouser pockets, so perhaps he was looking for something to eat.

No one was able to corner him. Passengers saw him for just

a blurred moment. He did not seem at all interested in humans. Well-dressed women crouched down, calling out high-pitched, artificial-sounding greetings, but he charged past them all without a pause and into the cherrywood cave of the library, and disappeared somewhere beyond that. Who could know what he was after? Or what he was feeling, in that no doubt pounding heart? He was just a hungry or scared dog on this claustrophobic ship whose alleyways suddenly became cul-de-sacs, as he ran farther and farther from any sign of daylight. Eventually the creature made his way trotting along a mahogany-panelled, carpeted hall and slipped through a half-open door into a master suite, as someone left it carrying a full tray. The dog jumped up onto an oversized bed, where Sir Hector de Silva lay, and bit down into his throat.

ALL NIGHT THE *ORONSAY* HAD BEEN WITHIN THE
protected waters of the Red Sea. At daybreak we passed the
small islands off Jizan, and we could see in the distance the hazy
presence of the oasis town of Abha, the sunlight revealing a
glint off a piece of glass or a white wall. Then the town dissolved
under the sun and was gone from our sight.

By breakfast the news of Sir Hector's death had already raced
over the ship, quickly followed by whispers that there would
have to be a burial at sea. But apparently a funeral could not
take place in coastal waters so the body would have to wait
for the open spaces of the Mediterranean. Next came the more
startling news of how he had died, followed by the story we
had already heard from the ayurvedic about the spell put on
him by the Buddhist priest. Ramadhin reasoned therefore it
was fate that had killed him, and not us, because we had
brought the dog on board. And as the little creature was never
to be seen again, we came to believe the smuggled dog was a
phantom.

During lunch most of the questions were to do with how
a dog had boarded the ship. And where was it now? Miss

Lasqueti was certain the Captain was in serious trouble. A lawsuit could be brought against him for negligence. Then Emily came over to our table and demanded to know if *we* had brought the dog onto the ship, and we responded with an attempted look of horror, which made her laugh. The only person showing no interest in the opinions around him was Mr Mazappa, who sat mulling over his oxtail soup. His musical fingers were for once still on the tablecloth. He seemed suddenly alone and incapable of talk, and he became my preoccupation during the meal, during all of the talk and conjectures about Sir Hector. I noticed Miss Lasqueti was also regarding him, her head lowered, gazing at him through the fence of her eyelashes. At one point she even put her hand over those still fingers, but he pulled his away. No, being within the stricter confines of the Red Sea was not an easy time for some of those at our table. Perhaps emotionally we felt landlocked after all the freedom that came with the wilder oceans we had crossed. And Death existed after all, or a more complicated idea of Fate. Doors were closing, it seemed, on our adventurous travels.

I WOKE THE NEXT MORNING WITHOUT THE USUAL DESIRE to meet with my friends. I heard Ramadhin's familiar knock, but I did not answer. Instead I took my time dressing, then went up to the deck alone. The desert light had been there for hours, and we passed Jeddah at about eight-thirty. On the other side of the ship passengers with binoculars were attempting to catch a glimpse of the Nile somewhere deep inland. They were all adults on the deck, no one I knew, and I felt without any connection. I tried to remember the cabin number for Emily, who was never an early riser, and I went there.

I was fondest of Emily when we were not surrounded by other people. In those moments, I always felt I learned from her. I knocked a couple of times before she opened the door, wrapped in a dressing gown. It was about nine by now, I had been awake for hours, but she had still been in bed.

'Oh, Michael.'

'Can I come in?'

'Yes.'

And she stalked back and slipped under the sheets, simultaneously discarding the robe, both done, it seemed, in the same movement.

'We are still in the Red Sea.'

'I know.'

'We went past Jeddah. I saw it.'

'If you are going to stay, make me some coffee, will you . . . ?'

'Do you want a cigarette?'

'Not yet.'

'When you do, can I light it?'

I stayed with her all morning. I do not know why I was confused about things. I was eleven. One doesn't know much then. I told her about the dog, how we had brought it on board. I was lying beside her on the bed, holding one of her unlit cigarettes, pretending to smoke, and she reached over and turned my head towards her.

'*Don't*,' she said. 'I mean, *don't* tell anyone else about this – what you just told me.'

'We think it might be a ghost,' I replied. 'The spell's ghost.'

'I don't care. You must not mention it again. Promise me.'

I said I wouldn't.

So began a tradition between us. That I would at certain moments in my life tell Emily things that I would not tell others. And later in our lives, much later, she would talk to me about what she had been going through. All through my life, Emily would be distinct from everyone I knew.

She touched the top of my head in a gesture that essentially managed to say, 'Oh, let's forget about it. Don't worry.' But I didn't turn away, and kept watching her.

'What?' She raised her eyebrow.

'I don't know, I feel strange. Being here. What will happen when I go to England? Will you be with me?'

'You know I won't.'

'But I don't know anyone there.'

'Your mother?'

'But I don't know her like I know you.'

'Yes you do.'

I put my head back on the pillow and looked up, no longer watching her.

'Mr Mazappa says I am peculiar.'

She laughed. 'You're not peculiar, Michael. Besides, that's not so bad.' She leaned over and kissed me. 'Now, make me some coffee. There's the cup. You can use hot water from the tap.' I got up and looked around.

'There's no coffee here.'

'Then order some.'

I pressed the intercom button and, while I waited, studied the photograph of the Queen of England watching us from the wall.

'Yes,' I said. 'Some coffee for cabin three-sixty. Miss Emily de Saram.'

When the steward arrived, I met him at the door, and when he left I brought the tray over for her. She half sat up, then remembered the robe and reached for it. But what I saw hit me at the base of my heart. There was a tremor within me, something that would be natural for me later but at that moment was a mixture of thrill and vertigo. Suddenly there was a wide gulf between Emily's existence and mine, and I would never be able to cross it.

If there was a desire of sorts in me, then where did it come from? Did it belong to another? Or was it a part of me? It was as if a hand from the desert that surrounded us had reached in and touched me. For the rest of my life it would recur, but in Emily's cabin it was my first brush with the long variety of it. Yet where had it come from? And was it a pleasure or a sadness, this life inside me? It was as if with its existence I was lacking something essential, like water. I put the tray down and climbed back onto Emily's high bed. I felt in that moment that I had been alone for years. I had existed too cautiously with my family, as though there had been shards of glass always around us.

And now I was going to England, where my mother had been living for three or four years. I don't remember how long she had been there. Even now, all these years later, I have not remembered that quite significant detail, the period of separation, as if, as for an animal, there was a limited knowledge of the span of missing time. Three days or three weeks is the same for a dog, they say. But when I return from any period of absence there is from my dog a courteous instant recognition as we embrace and wrestle on the carpeted floor of the front hall; and yet, when I did meet my mother eventually, on the docks at Tilbury, she had already become 'another', a stranger, whose fold

I would cautiously enter. There was no doglike embrace or tussle or familiar smell. And I think this may have been because of what occurred with Emily – our distantly related selves – that morning in that ochre-coloured cabin, shuttered away from the dazzle of the Red Sea and the desert that stretched away for miles.

I knelt on that bed on my hands and knees and shook. Emily leaned forward and embraced me, in so soft a gesture I felt barely touched, an envelope of loose air between us. My hot tears that had come from my darkness rubbed on her cool upper arm.

'What is it?'

'I don't know.' Whatever small props of necessary defence I'd surrounded myself with, which contained and protected me, and which had marked the outline of me, were no longer there.

Perhaps we talked then. I don't remember. I was conscious of the easy quietness around me, my breathing eventually at the same calm pace of her breathing.

I must have fallen asleep for a moment, and woke when Emily, not moving away from me, reached her other hand over her shoulder in a backstroke gesture for the cup of coffee. And soon I heard the quick swallows, my ear against her neck. Her other hand was still gripping mine as no one had ever done, convincing me of a security that probably did not exist.

Adults are always prepared for the gradual or sudden swerve in an oncoming story. Like the Baron, Mr Mazappa would get off the boat when our ship reached Port Said and disappear from our lives – he had been overpowered by something in the few days before reaching Aden. And Mr Daniels would become aware that Emily had no interest in him or his world of plants. And the millionaire's death from his second dog bite was more tragic than exciting. Even our unfortunate Captain would continue his journey and find more chaos among his human cargo. They all must have been imprisoned or fated in some way. But for me, in that cabin, it was the first time I looked at myself with a distant eye, just as the neutral eyes of the distant young Queen had watched me all morning.

When I left Emily's room (and there was to be no repeat of this intimacy), I knew I would always be linked to her, by some underground river or a seam of coal or silver – well, let us say silver, because she has always been important to me. In the Red Sea, I must have fallen in love with her. Though when I pulled away, the magnet of it, whatever *it* was, had gone.

How long was I in what felt like that sky-high bed with Emily? When we've met it is never mentioned. She may not even recall how much of my grief she took away or held on to, or for how long. I had never known the grip of another, or the smell of an arm that had just emerged from sleep. I had never wept beside someone who also excited me in a way I could not fathom. But there must have been an understanding in her as she looked down at me, and in her small courteous gestures.

Writing this, I do not want it to end until I can understand it better, in a way that would calm me even now, all these years later. For instance, how far did our intimacy go? I don't know. It was, I believe, nothing of much importance to Emily. It was probably a casual if genuine kindness she gave me – and saying that takes nothing away from her gesture. 'You should go now,' she said, and rose from the bed and walked to the bathroom and closed the door behind her.

Broken heart, you
timeless wonder.

What a small
place to be.

'MY DREAMS,' EMILY SAYS, LEANING FORWARD ACROSS THE table that separates us. 'You would not want to know them, they are— I am surrounded by their darkness, the incessant danger. Clouds crash against each other, loudly. Does this happen to you?'

We were in London, some years later.

'No,' I say. 'I rarely dream. I don't seem to. Perhaps they emerge as daydreams.'

'Every night I go into them, and I wake up afraid.'

What was strange about this fear, almost guilt, was Emily's ease with others during the day. It felt to me there was never darkness in her, there was instead the desire to comfort. Who or what caused this darkness in her? Now and then there would be a sense of separateness, when she seemed to give up on the world around her. And at those times she had an unreachable face. So for a while there was her 'distance'. But when she returned to you, it was a gift.

Early on she had confessed a pleasure in danger. She was right about that. It was there like a joker, something that did not quite fit in her nature. There were always to be discoveries about her, some of them as small as that wink on the pier in Aden when she wanted me to guess at something. But a good part of her world, as I would come to know later, long after our time on the *Oronsay*, she kept to herself, and I have come to realise the gentleness of manner I spoke of must have grown naturally out of a disguised life.

Kennels

I WOKE THE NEXT MORNING TO FIND MR HASTIE STILL
in bed, reading a novel. 'Good morning, young man,' he said,
hearing me jump down from my top bunk. 'Off with your
pals?'

There had been no card game the night before, and I was
curious as to why. Although since the millionaire's death, many
schedules and habits seemed to have been altered. Now Mr
Hastie proceeded to inform me he had been relieved of his
duties. He was no longer in charge of the kennels. The Captain
had been looking for someone to blame and now believed it
was one of the hounds from Mr Hastie's kennels that had
escaped its cage, slipped into the Emperor Class cabin, and
bitten Hector de Silva to death. Since the man's death, a curious
thing was occurring. The de Silva knighthood seemed to
have fallen away, and was no longer mentioned. People began
referring to him as 'the dead man'. The knighthood was turning
out to be as mortal as the body.

I stood in front of Mr Hastie, listening with sympathy to
this false accusation, but did not say a word. The little mongrel
from Aden had not been found. The demotion of Mr Hastie

meant he would now be on paint-and-varnish duty in the noonday sun, while his kennel assistant and fellow bridge player, Mr Invernio, took charge of the dogs. 'I wonder how he is getting on with the O'Neal Weimaraner?' Mr Hastie murmured.

Later that day, after a random search for Ramadhin's dog, the three of us strolled over to the kennels. Out on B Deck, along their twenty-yard runway, were several dogs moving slowly, as if with sunstroke, blank looks on their faces. We climbed over the barrier and walked into the kennels, where every dog was barking to be let out. Invernio was trying to read one of Hastie's books in the midst of the racket. He recognised me when we came up to him, having seen my head peer down at him from the top bunk, and I introduced him to Cassius and Ramadhin. He put down *The Bhagavad Gita* and walked around the kennels with us, flinging pieces of meat at those who were his favourites. Then he brought out the Weimaraner. He removed the collar, stroked the grey egg-smooth head, and ordered the dog to walk away from him, to the far end of the mote-filled room. The dog was not eager to leave Invernio's company but followed the commands of *'Get! Get! Get! Get!'* walking away silently, its long legs tossing themselves to the left and to the right. At the far end of the kennel the dog turned and waited. *'Hola!'* Invernio yelled, and the dog charged towards him in a slim gallop and when two yards from him leapt for his head. All four paws simultaneously landed on Invernio's shoulders and chest, hard enough that the kennel keeper fell back, the dog overpowering him with scrabbling claws and loud barking.

Invernio struggled to get on top of the animal and growled into the creature's ear. Then he started kissing the dog, which responded like a woman who loved the kisser but did not want to be kissed. They rolled over each other several times. It took only a second to recognise the affection. Both of them were clearly besotted with each other. They bared their teeth. They laughed and barked. Invernio blew into the dog's nose. All the caged dogs were now silent, watching enviously as the two of them roughhoused in the dust.

We left in mid-competition, and I went off alone to C Deck and stayed there for most of the afternoon. Mr Invernio and the dog had reminded me too much of our cook, Gunepala, and I was missing him, how he was always attended by a lunatic choir of rice hounds at mealtimes, howling in unison as he waved a piece of meat to and fro before eventually flinging it into their midst. In the afternoons I would come across him asleep with them in his arms. At least Gunepala slept, while the dogs lay politely beside him watching one another, twitching and raising their eyebrows.

THE PRISONER'S NIGHT WALKS RESUMED. WE DID NOT see him between the night before landing in Aden and the evening we left the city. There must have been some reason he had been kept in his cell. Now, as we travelled farther north in the Red Sea, we saw that an extra chain had been added, linking the metal collar at his neck to a strut bolted to the deck twelve yards away. We saw him shuffle up and down. Before, he had moved as if a nimble man, but now he appeared hesitant and cautious. Perhaps he sensed a different world out there, for one could distinguish the night shores of the desert on either side of the ship – Arabia to our right, and Egypt to our left.

Emily had whispered to me that the prisoner's name was Niemeyer, something like that. It sounded too European, for he was clearly Asian. He looked a mixture of Sinhalese and something else. We overheard him speaking to a guard. It was a deep, calm voice, and he was slow with his words. Ramadhin thought it was a voice that could hypnotise you if you were alone in a room with him. My friend imagined all sorts of dangers. But Emily also mentioned his distinctive voice. She'd been told by someone that it was 'convincing' but 'scary'. Though when I asked who had told her, she clammed up. I was surprised. I felt I was enough of a confidant to be trusted by her. Then she added, 'It is someone else's secret. Not mine. I can't give it to you, all right?'

In any case, Niemeyer's return to our deck for his nocturnal walks made us feel that some order had been restored. And we began to camp in one of the lifeboats, in order to look down at him. We listened to the hellish chains scrape the deck. He would pause at the end of his tether and look into the night as if he could clearly make out what was there, as if there were a person miles away in the black of the desert who was witnessing his every move. Then he'd turn and come back along the same path. Eventually they unpinned the iron collar from his neck. We heard some quiet words back and forth between him and the guards, and he was led below deck to a place we could only imagine.

'ATTENTION STRETCHER PARTY, STRETCHER PARTY — PROCEED TO BADMINTON COURT ON A DECK.' We ran to the source of the urgency. This was one of the more interesting announcements we had heard so far from the loudspeakers. More often they announced afternoon lectures in the Clyde Room about 'The Laying of the Undersea Cables Between Aden and Bombay', or that a Mr Blackler would speak on 'A Recent Reconstruction of Mozart's Piano'. Before *The Four Feathers* had been screened, a chaplain had given a talk titled 'The Crusades, Pro and Con: Did England Go Too Far?' Ramadhin and Mr Fonseka went to that lecture and returned to tell us that apparently the speaker felt the English did not go far enough.

A NEW RUMOUR PERCOLATED DOWN THAT THE DAYS-OLD corpse of Hector de Silva would soon be buried at sea. The Captain wished to wait until we reached the Mediterranean, but the all-powerful de Silva widow was now insisting on a quick, private burial. And so, within the space of an hour everyone had discovered the location and time of the ceremony. Stewards roped off a section of the stern where the service would take place, but gawkers soon assembled behind the rope and crowded the metal stairways, and looked down from the higher-deck levels. A few less impressed souls regarded the proceedings through the windows of the smoking room. As a result, the body – really the first sighting of Hector de Silva for most of us – had to be carried along a very narrow aisle, grudgingly allowed by the crowd. It was followed by his widow, his daughter, his three doctors (one of them dressed in full village regalia), and the Captain.

I had never been to a funeral, let alone one for which I was partially responsible. I saw Emily a few yards away and got a cautious look from her that included a slight shake of the head. I saw the Baron standing quite close to the de Silva family.

Everyone from the Cat's Table was there. Even Mr Fonseka had left his cabin and come up for the ceremony. He stood next to us dressed in a black coat and tie, something he had probably bought in Kundanmals in the Fort for his English sojourn.

We looked down at the small figures of the entourage, surrounding the trestle table that held the bust of Hector de Silva and some flowers. We were barely able to hear the last rites. The voice of the priest faltered and disappeared in the shuddering winds coming from across the desert. When the family approached the body wrapped in its white shroud, all of us leaned forward to witness whatever secret was being passed to the dead. Then Hector de Silva slid from the ship and disappeared into the sea. There were no rifle shots or cannon fire, as Cassius had promised. Nothing further was done or said to end the ceremony. Only Mr Fonseka recited something quietly to those beside him. *'Who hath desired the sea? Her excellent loneliness rather / Than the forecourts of kings.'* He spoke Kipling's lines in such a way that they sounded grand and wise to us. We were not aware of its irony in the context of Hector de Silva's life.

Another teatime lecture was given a few hours later, to prepare us for the Suez Canal: on de Lesseps, and about the thousands of workers who died from cholera during its construction, as well as on the Canal's present importance as a trade route. Ramadhin and I arrived early and scoured the buffet tables for the best sandwiches, which were supposed to be eaten only when the talk had ended. In mid-lecture I ran into Flavia Prins with two of her card-playing associates, while I was walking away from the food tables with several sandwiches balanced along my arm. She took in everything with a faltering of her eyes and walked past me without saying a word.

WE APPROACHED THE CANAL IN DARKNESS, AT THE STROKE
of midnight. A few passengers camped on the decks to take
in the experience were half asleep, scarcely conscious of the
clangs and bells that guided our ship into the narrow eye of
the needle that was El Suweis. We paused to take on an Arab
harbour pilot who climbed from his barge up a rope ladder.
He walked slowly towards the bridge, ignoring all authority
around him. This was his property now. He would be the one
to take us into even shallower waters and adjust the angle of
the ship so we could slip into the narrower canal on which we
would travel the 190 kilometres to Port Said. We could see
him in the brightly lit horizontal windows of the bridge beside
the Captain and two other officers.

It was the night we never slept.

In less than half an hour we were sidling alongside a concrete
dock with crates stacked into giant pyramids and men running
with electrical cables and baggage carts alongside the slow-
moving *Oronsay*. Everywhere there was fast, intense work under
the pockets of sulphurous light. We could hear shouts and
whistles, and in one of the intervals we heard barking that

made Ramadhin think it was his dog from Aden, who was now attempting to get back to shore. The three of us hung over the railings, gulping in air, taking it in. This night turned out to be our most vivid memory of the journey, the time I stumble upon now and then in a dream. We were not active, but a constantly changing world slid past our ship, the darkness various and full of suggestion. Unseen tractors were grinding along the abutments. The cranes bent low, poised to pluck one of us off as we passed. We had crossed open seas at twenty-two knots, and now we moved as if hobbled, at the speed of a slow bicycle, as if within the gradual unrolling of a scroll.

Bundles were being flung up onto the foredeck. A rope had been fastened to the railing so a sailor could swing himself down to the passing land to sign territorial papers. I saw a painting leave the ship. In my sidelong glimpse it appeared familiar, I might have seen it in one of the First Class lounges. Why would a painting be removed from the ship? I could not tell whether everything taking place was carefully legal or a frenzy of criminality, for only a few officials oversaw what was going on, and all the deck lights were out and all activity was hushed. There were just the lit windows of the bridge, with the three constant silhouettes, as if puppets guided the ship, following the orders of the harbour pilot. He came out a few times onto the open deck and whistled into the night to instruct a man he recognised onshore. A concurring whistle replied and we'd hear the splash of a dropped chain and the bow of the ship would jerk suddenly, to re-angle itself to one side or the other. Ramadhin kept running up and down the length of the ship in search of his dog. Cassius and I perched precariously on the bow railing, where we could witness the fragmentary tableaux below us – a merchant with his stall of food, engineers talking by a bonfire, the unloading of refuse, all of them, all of this, we knew we would never see again. So we came to understand that small and important thing, that our lives could be large with interesting strangers who would pass us without any personal involvement.

I remember still how we moved in that canal, our visibility muted, and those sounds that were messages from shore, and the sleepers on deck missing this panorama of activity. We were on the railing bucking up and down. We could have fallen and lost our ship and begun another fate – as paupers or as princes. *'Uncle!'* we shouted, if someone was close enough to distinguish our small figures. *'Hullo, Uncle!'* And people would wave, fling us a grin. Everyone who saw us sliding by was an uncle that night. Someone threw us an orange. An orange from the desert! Cassius kept shouting for beedis, but they did not understand him. A dockworker held up something, a plant or an animal, but the darkness disguised it too well.

No other vessel would be travelling that night in the Canal's dark waters. Radio contact had been at work for more than a day so that we would enter, as we had to, at the very moment of midnight. Under a swaying cord of electrical light, down there onshore, was a man sitting at a makeshift table, filling out forms he handed to a runner who caught up with the ship and flung the papers with a metal weight so they landed at the feet of one of the sailors. We never stopped moving, we passed the runner, as well as the man at the table furiously recording the charts of exchange, and a canteen cook beside an open fire roasting a thing whose odour was a gift, a desire in the night, a temptation to abandon the ship after all the European food we had been eating for days. Cassius said, 'That is what frankincense smells like.' And so our ship continued, guided by these strangers. We were collecting what was fresh from the land, bartering for objects thrown on board. Who knows what was exchanged that night, and what cross-fertilisation occurred as the legal papers of entrance and exit were signed and passed back down to land, while we entered and left the brief and temporary world of El Suweis.

We drifted into morning light. Clotted clouds speckled the sky. We hadn't seen clouds for our whole journey, save the dark mountains of them that banked above our ship and fell upon us during the storms. Then, approaching Port Said, a sandstorm rose up and hung over us, a last gasp from Arabia that caused havoc with the ship's radar signals. This was the reason our arrival at El Suweis had been carefully timed to begin at midnight – in order that we would reach Port Said in daylight, when navigation could be based on what could be seen with human sight. So we entered the Mediterranean with our eyes wide open.

*

THERE WAS A TIME IN MY LATE TWENTIES WHEN I suddenly had an urge to meet with Cassius again. While I had kept in touch with and spent time with Ramadhin and his family, I had not seen Cassius since the day our ship docked in England.

And during this period when I had the desire to see him, I came across an announcement in a London newspaper. There was a photograph of him. I would not have recognised the face except that it had his name beside it. Older, darker, as different as I probably was from the boy I had been on board that ship in the 1950s. It was an advertisement for a show of his paintings. And so I went into the city, to a gallery on Cork Street. I went there not so much to see his art as to make contact with him, to have, I hoped, a long meal together and talk and talk and talk. I knew little of what had happened to him since our three weeks together, although I knew he had become a well-considered painter. That had surprised me. But was he as wild, I wondered. And had he remained as dangerous as he had seemed to me when I was a boy? Some grains of Cassius had, after all, remained in my system. I looked again at the announcement I had cut out of the newspaper, at the picture of him leaning against a white wall with a hint of belligerence.

But Cassius was not there. It was a Saturday afternoon. I got to the gallery and was told the show had opened a few evenings earlier and that Cassius had made his appearance then. I did not know much about the habits of the art world. It was a disappointment, but his absence did not matter. For what I saw in the paintings was Cassius himself. They were large canvasses that filled the three rooms of the Waddington Gallery. About fifteen of them. They were all about that night in El Suweis. The very same sulphur lights above the night activity that I still remembered, or at least began to remember that Saturday afternoon. And the open fires. The ancient-looking logbook being filled urgently by the scribe at the table in the crisp night air. I had thought the paintings were abstractions at first. There was a sense in them that things were taking place on the edge of or just beyond the painted colours. But once I knew where we were, everything altered. I even found Ramadhin's small dog gazing up at the boat. All this enlarged me, and I did not know why. I suppose it clarified how close Cassius and I had been, real brothers. For he also had witnessed the people I saw that night, with whom we had felt so oddly aligned, whom we would never see again. Only there. In that night city of another world. We had not talked of this, but it had somehow come to both of us. And now they were here with us.

I walked over to the visitors' book, where people were expected to write comments. Some of them were quite grand, overly intellectual, some just said 'Delightful!' A loose scrawl that took over a whole page said, 'LITTLE OLD LADY GOT MUTILATED LATE LAST NIGHT.' It must have been written by one of Cassius's drunken friends. No one else had written on that page, and the sentence exposed itself there, quite solitary. I leafed through the rest of the pages for a while and came across Miss Lasqueti's name, with a sweet praising of Cassius's art. I put down the date, and I wrote: 'The Oronsay tribe – irresponsible and wiolent.' Then I added, 'Sorry to miss you. Mynah.' I left no address.

I went outside but something else held me, so I decided to walk through the gallery again, this time glad there was hardly anyone else there. And when I understood what it was that drew me, I circled the gallery once more, to make sure. I read somewhere that when people first celebrated the distinct point of view of Lartigue's early photographs, it took a while before someone pointed out that it was the natural angle of a small boy with a camera looking *up* at the adults he was photographing. What I was seeing now in the gallery was the exact angle of vision Cassius and I had that night, from the railing, looking down at the men working in those pods of light. An angle of forty-five degrees, something like that. I was back on the railing, watching, which was where Cassius was emotionally, when he was doing these paintings. Goodbye, we were saying to all of them. Goodbye.

Ramadhin's Heart

FOR MOST OF MY LIFE I HAVE KNOWN THERE WAS NOTHING I could give Cassius that would be of any use to him. But I felt I could have given something to Ramadhin. He allowed me affection. There was a bitter appeal for Cassius about his own privacy. I saw it even in the paintings, in spite of his evocation of that night in El Suweis. But I always thought I could have helped Ramadhin in a difficult situation. If I had known. If he had come and talked to me.

In the early 1970s, while I was working for a brief period in North America, I received a cable from a distant relative. I remember it was my thirtieth birthday. Leaving what I was doing, I managed to get on a red-eye flight to London, where I checked into a hotel and slept for a few hours.

At noon I took a taxi that dropped me off in Mill Hill, by a small chapel. I caught a brief glimpse of Ramadhin's sister, Massi, and then, once we were inside, of her coming down the aisle. Since our teenage friendship we had not seen much of each other. I had in fact not seen Ramadhin or any members of his family for eight years. I suspected we had all become very different people. Ramadhin had written in one of his last letters to me that Massi was 'moving with a fast coterie' and working for the BBC, on one of its music shows, and that she was ambitious and very smart. Nothing about Massi would have surprised me, I suppose. She was younger, and had arrived in England a year after us and quickly adapted.

Over the years, I had come to know their parents well, a gentle pair who had brought up that very gentle son. The father was a biologist, and he always spoke about my uncle, 'The Judge', whenever he found himself forced to have a chat with me when no one else was around. I suppose my uncle and Ramadhin's father were at about the same career level. Mr Ramadhin, though, was a slightly incompetent man in terms of the real world (wrenches, breakfast, timetables), while his wife, also a biologist, organised everything and seemed to be content standing in the shadow he cast. Their life and their careers and their home were to be a ladder for their children to climb up on. And in my teens I wanted to spend as much time as I could in the quiet discipline and calm of their Mill Hill house. I was always there. Ramadhin's illness, his heart trouble, had made them a more cautious and quieter family than mine. They existed under a bell jar. I was at ease with them.

Now I was back in that very same landscape. And walking to the Ramadhins' home after the funeral made me feel I was falling through branches we had climbed years earlier. The house, when I got there, looked smaller, and Mrs Ramadhin looked frail. The wisps of white hair made her taut face more beautiful, more forgiving – for she had been a strict as well as a generous person to her children and to me. It was only Massi who could fight against her mother's rules, as she did for a good part of her life.

'You stayed away too long, Michael. You stay away all the time.' The mother's words were an arrow carefully pointed at me, before she came forward and let me enclose her in my arms. In the past, we had barely touched. 'Mrs R.' I had called her all through my teenage years.

So once again I entered their home on Terracotta Road. A group of people were giving their condolences to the parents in the narrow hallway and then walking on towards the living room, where the sofa and the nest of side tables and the paintings were in the very same places they had been when I visited as a teenager. It was a time capsule of our youth – the small television set, the same portraits of Ramadhin's grandparents in front of their home in Mutwal. The past his family had brought to this country would never be given up. But now there was an added picture on the mantelpiece, of Ramadhin in his graduation robes at Leeds University. The plumage did not suit him or disguise him. His face looked gaunt, as if he was under stress.

I had walked up close to it and was staring at him. Someone gripped my arm at the elbow, fingers pressing intentionally hard into the flesh, and I turned. It was Massi, and suddenly, almost too quickly, it felt we were shockingly close to each other. I had seen her at the chapel when she'd walked between her parents to sit in the front row and quickly bent her head down. She had not been in the receiving line in the hall.

'You came, Michael. I didn't think you would come.'

'Why wouldn't I?' Her warm, small hand touched my face,

and then she was off to deal with others, to speak and nod to what was being said to her, or give a needed embrace. She was all I watched. I was looking for any sign of Ramadhin in her. There had never been much echo between them. He was large, had a lumbering body, while she was taut and quick. A 'fast coterie', he had written. They had the same colour hair, that was all. But I felt there must be something she now carried of him – something she had been given at his abrupt departure. I suppose I needed Ramadhin's presence, and it was not here.

It would be a long afternoon, during which we saw each other only from across the room, speaking to various relatives. All through the stand-up lunch I noticed her moving from person to person in this expatriate community in the role of a dutiful family bee – going from a devastated old aunt, to an uncle still too cheerful by habit, to a nephew who did not understand why everyone was so calm, for he adored Ramadhin, who had tutored him in mathematics and used to reason with him through any crisis. I saw her sitting with that boy on a lounge chair in the garden, and I wanted to be there with them rather than under the curious gaze of one of her parents' friends. I suppose because the boy was ten years old. And I wished to know what she was saying to him, how she could justify what she was saying or why we were behaving like some composed sect who spoke only in whispers. And then I saw it was not the boy who was weeping but Massi.

I left the man in mid-sentence and went out and sat by her and put my arm around her shuddering body that never stopped shaking, and not one of the three of us thought of speaking. And when I looked up later through the glass doors into the house, I realised that all the adults were inside and we were the children in the garden.

The evening began to darken and as it did, the Ramadhins' modest home, which had once been a sanctuary for me, seemed a frail ark. The last visitors were slowly walking out onto the unlit suburban street. I was standing beside the family in the hallway about to leave as well, needing to make the train back to central London.

'I have to catch a plane tomorrow afternoon,' I said, 'but I'll be back in a month, with luck.'

Massi was watching me carefully. It was what we both had been doing all afternoon, as if reconsidering a person we had once known well. Her face was broader and there was a different manner than when we were young. I was witnessing her new and careful courtesy to her parents. She who had been in loud battle with them all through her teens. I was aware of these differences just as I knew she could pin me down more clearly than anyone among my recent friends. She could have hauled out some perception of me from our past and placed it adjacent to what she was seeing now. She'd been the sidekick to her brother and me during school holidays, when the three of us lounged in a city that was not quite ours and where we were made to feel it was not quite ours — it was a strange contained universe we moved around in, taking the bus to a swimming pool in Bromley or to the Croydon public library, or to Earls Court to see the Boat Show, or Dog Show, or Motor Show. No doubt we still had the same knowledge of those specific bus routes in our brains. She'd witnessed all my changes during our teens. All of this was in her.

Then the gap of eight years.

'I have to catch a plane tomorrow afternoon but I'll be back in a month, with luck.'

She stood in the hallway watching me, her face in clear shock at the loss of her brother. Her boyfriend was beside her, holding her by the elbow. We had spoken earlier in the evening. If he was not her boyfriend, he certainly hoped to be.

'Well, let me know when you get back,' Massi said.

'I will.'

'Massi, why don't you walk with Michael to the station? You two should talk,' Mrs R. said.

'Yes, come with me,' I said. 'This way we'll have an hour together.'

'A lifetime,' she said.

Massi existed in the public half of the world that Ramadhin rarely entered. There was never hesitation in her. She and I would come to share a deep slice of each other's lives. And whatever became of our relationship, the ups and downs of its seas, we improved as well as damaged each other with the quickness I learned partially from her. Massi grabbed at decisions. She was probably more like Cassius than like her brother. Although I know now that the world is not divided that simply into two natures. But in our youth we think that.

'A lifetime,' she had said. And in that hour I took the first steps back into Massi's life. The two of us walked to the station and our pace slowed as we spoke. We entered total darkness where the road bordered a soccer field, and it felt we were whispering in an unlit corner of a stage. We talked mostly about her. She already knew enough about me, my brief, surprising career that had taken me to North America, and resulted in my leaving her world. (*I didn't think you would come.* '*You stay away all the time.*') We excavated the missing years. I had hardly been in touch, even with Ramadhin. I sent an occasional postcard that located where I was, nothing much more than that. There was a lot to discover about what she and her brother had been doing.

'Do you know of a person named Heather Cave?' she asked.

'No. Should I? Who is she?' I imagined some person I might have run into in America or Canada.

'Apparently Ramadhin knew her.'

She went on to say there had been no convincing explanation for the circumstances of Ramadhin's death. He had been found with his heart stopped, a knife beside him. That was all. He had gone into the darkness of one of the communal gardens in the city, near the girl's flat. Massi told me he was supposedly obsessed with her, someone he had been tutoring. But when Massi looked into it, there was only one girl, fourteen years old, Heather Cave, who he gave lessons to. If she was the one Ramadhin was enamoured of, he would have had an overwhelming guilt that must have filled him like dark ink.

She shook her head and turned away from the subject.

She said she did not believe her brother's existence in England had been happy; she felt he would have been more content with a career and a home in Colombo.

Every immigrant family, it seems, has someone who does not belong in the new country they have come to. It feels like permanent exile to that one brother or wife who cannot stand a silent fate in Boston or London or Melbourne. I've met many who remain haunted by the persistent ghost of an earlier place. And it *is* true that Ramadhin's life would have been happier in the more casual and less public world of Colombo. He had no professional ambition, as Massi did and, as she suspected, I did. He was the more gradual one, the more concerned one, who learned what was important at his own pace. I told her I still wondered how he had managed to put up with Cassius and me on that voyage to England. She was nodding, smiling now, and then asked, 'Have you seen him? I read about him every so often.'

'Remember we told you once that you should look him up?'

We began to laugh. At one time, Ramadhin and I had tried to convince Massi that Cassius would be the perfect person for her to marry.

'Maybe I should . . . maybe I still could.' She was kicking at the wet leaves in front of her, and had put her arm through mine. I thought about my other missing friend. The last time I had heard about Cassius was when I met an actress from Sri Lanka who knew him when they were teenagers in England. She spoke of how he took her on a date, very early in the morning, to a golf course. He brought along a couple of old clubs, a few balls, and they climbed over the gate and wandered on the course, Cassius smoking a joint and lecturing her on the greatness of Nietzsche before he attempted to seduce her on one of the greens.

At the station we confirmed the time of the train, then went into the night café under the railway bridge and sat there barely speaking, looking at each other across the formica.

I never categorised Massi as Ramadhin's sister. They seemed too distinctly themselves. She had an eager spirit. One mentioned a possibility and she met it, like the next line of a song. She was someone people in another era would have called 'a pistol'. That is how Mr Mazappa or Miss Lasqueti would have described her. But she was inward and hesitant this night in the almost empty cafeteria by the train station. There was an older couple there, who had also been at the funeral and reception, but they kept to themselves. I needed Ramadhin there, with us. I was used to that. Maybe it was Massi's quietness that allowed his presence, and maybe it was this new affection between us that so quickly erased the years, but he came right into my heart and I started crying. Everything about him was suddenly there in me: his slow stroll, his awkwardness around a questionable joke, his love and need of that dog in Aden, his careful care of his heart – 'Ramadhin's heart' – the knots he had tied and was so proud of that had saved our lives, how his body looked when he walked away from you. And the decent intelligence that Mr Fonseka saw, and that Cassius and I never saw or acknowledged, but which was always there. How much more of Ramadhin did I take into myself, just with memory, after we stopped seeing each other?

I am someone who has a cold heart. If I am beside a great grief I throw barriers up so the loss cannot go too deep or too far. There is a wall instantly in place, and it will not fall. Proust has this line: 'We think we no longer love our dead, but . . .

suddenly we catch sight again of an old glove and burst into tears.' I don't know what it was. There was no glove. He had been dead six days. If I was being honest, I had to admit I had not really thought of Ramadhin as someone I had been close to for some time. In our twenties we are busy becoming other people.

Did I feel guilty that I had not loved him enough? That was partly it. But it was not any thought that broke down the wall, allowing him to come into me. I must have begun remembering, replaying all the little fragments of him that revealed the concern he had for me. A gesture to signal that I was spilling something on my shirt, which in fact had happened the last time I saw him. The way he tried to include me in what he was excitedly learning. How he went out of his way to hunt me down and then remain my friend in England, when he had gone to one school and I to another. I was not difficult to find in the network of expatriates, but anyway he had searched me out.

I have no idea how long I sat like that, by the plate-glass window that separated me from the street, with Massi across from me not saying a word, just her hand reaching out to me, palm turned up, that I did not see and so had not taken. We are expanded by tears, we are told, not reduced by them. It had taken me a long time. I couldn't look at her. I peered beyond the fall of restaurant light into the dark.

'Come. Come with me,' she said, and we went up the stone steps of the station to wait for the train. There were still a few minutes and we walked up and down the long platform to its unlit peripheries and back, not a word between us. When the train approached there would be an embrace, a kiss of recognition and sadness that would knock down the door for us for the next few years. We heard the crackle of an announcement and then saw one light beaming down on us.

SOME EVENTS TAKE A LIFETIME TO REVEAL THEIR damage and influence. I see now that I married Massi to stay close to a community from childhood I felt safe in and, I realised, still wished for.

Massi and I continued to see each other, at first shyly, and then partially to recover the almost lovers we had been in our teens. There was the shared grief of Ramadhin's death. And then there was the comfort of family. Her parents welcomed me back into their home – the boy, still a boy to them, who had been for years their son's best friend. So I would often go to Mill Hill and be in the house that I once had escaped to as a teenager, where I used to loaf with Ramadhin and his sister while their parents were at work – in their living room with its television, or in the upstairs bedroom with the green foliage outside. It is a place I could walk through blindfolded, even now – my arms outstretched to gauge the width of the hall, taking so many steps to enter that room by the garden, then three more steps to the right, avoiding the low table, so I would know, when I slipped the blindfold off, that I would be standing in front of the graduation picture of Ramadhin.

There was no one else and no other place I could turn to with my emptiness.

A month after his death, Ramadhin's family received a consoling letter from Mr Fonseka and they allowed me to read it, for he described our days on the *Oronsay*. He did say some polite words about me (and nothing about Cassius), and he spoke of seeing 'a luminous academic curiosity' in Ramadhin. He wrote about how the two of them had discussed the histories of the various countries we had travelled past, and all the natural as opposed to the artificial harbours; how Aden had been one of the thirteen great pre-Islamic cities; how there was an ancestry of famous Muslim geographers who'd lived there before the age of the gunpowder empires. On and on Fonseka's letter went, in a style that was still familiar to me almost twenty years later.

Fonseka's passion for knowledge always had within it the added pleasure of his sharing it. It was the way I suppose Ramadhin was with the ten-year-old nephew he had tutored whom I had met at the funeral. Mr Fonseka would not have known I was still in touch with the Ramadhin family, and I suppose I could have surprised him by going up to Sheffield with Massi to visit him. But I never did. She and I were busy most weekends. We were lovers again now, engaged to be married, with all of the formality that families who live abroad insist on. The weight of the tradition of exiles had fallen over us. Still, we should have skipped all of that, rented a car, and gone to see him. But I would have been shy of him at that stage in my life. I was a young writer and feared his response, even though I am sure he would have been courteous. It was after all Ramadhin who he must have assumed had the natural sensitivity and intelligence to be an artist. I do not believe those are necessary requisites, but I half believed it then.

I am still surprised it was Cassius and I who came out of that world and survived in the world of art. Cassius, who in his public persona insisted on using only his argumentative first name. I was more amiable, I had cleaned up my act, but Cassius took it on the road, scorning, snorting at the pooh-bahs of art and power. A few years after he had become well-known, his school in England, which he had hated and which had probably disliked him, asked him to donate a painting. He cabled back, 'FUCK YA! STRONG LETTER FOLLOWS.' He was always one of the roughs. Whenever I heard of something outrageous and thrilling that Cassius had done, I simultaneously thought of Fonseka reading about it in the newspapers and sighing at the gulf that existed between fairness and art.

I *should* have gone to see him, our old guru of the hemp smoke. He would have revealed Ramadhin in a different way from how Massi did. But her family had been broken, and she and I were the link to mend it, or at least plaster over the uncertain situation of his death that had left all of them powerless in dealing with their grief. As well, our desires were fed by an earlier time, from that very early morning in our youth when she seemed painted by those shifting green branches. We all have an old knot in the heart we wish to loosen and untie.

Being sisterless and brotherless, I had behaved with Ramadhin and Massi as if they were my siblings. It was the kind of relationship one has only during one's teens, as opposed to the kind of relationship with those we collide against when older – with whom we are more likely to change our lives.

So I thought.

Together the three of us had crossed those abstract and seemingly uncharted times that were the summer and winter holidays. We'd skulked around the universe of Mill Hill. At the cycle track we reenacted great races – wobbling up the slope, charging down the incline to a sensational photo finish. In the afternoon we disappeared into some *bijou* in central London to watch a film. Our universe included Battersea Power Station, the Pelican Stairs in Wapping that led down into the Thames, the Croydon library, the Chelsea public baths and Streatham Common, sloping from the High Road towards distant trees. (This was where Ramadhin found himself for a while on the last night of his life.) And Colliers Water Lane, where Massi and I eventually lived together. All these places she and Ramadhin and I had entered as teenagers and come out of as adults. But what did we really know, even of one another? We never thought of a future. Our small solar system – what was it heading towards? And how long would each of us mean something to the others?

*

SOMETIMES WE FIND OUR TRUE AND INHERENT SELVES during youth. It is a recognition of something that at first is small within us, that we will grow into somehow. My shipboard nickname was 'Mynah'. Almost my name but with a step into the air and a glimpse of some extra thing, like the slight swivel in their walk all birds have when they travel by land. Also it is an unofficial bird, and unreliable, its voice not fully trustworthy in spite of the range. At that time, I suppose, I was the mynah of the group, repeating whatever I overheard to the other two. Ramadhin gave it to me accidentally, and Cassius, recognising its easy outgrowth from my name, started calling me that.

No one called me 'Mynah' but the two friends I made on the *Oronsay*. Once I entered school in England, I was known only by my surname. But if I ever got a phone call and someone said 'Mynah,' it could be only one of them.

As for Ramadhin's own first name, I rarely used it, though I knew it. Does knowing give me permission to assume I understand most things about him? Do I have the right to imagine the processes of thought he went through as an adult? No. But as boys on that journey to England, looking out on the sea that seemed to contain nothing, we used to imagine complex plots and stories for ourselves.

Ramadhin's heart. Ramadhin's dog. Ramadhin's sister. Ramadhin's girl. It is only now that I see the various milestones in my life that connected the two of us. The dog, for instance. I still recall our playing with it on the narrow bunk bed during the brief time it was with us. And how it had at one moment come over to me quietly and fit its snout and jaws between my shoulder and neck like a violin. Its scared warmth. And then with Massi, our fitting together too, cautious and nervous as teenagers, and then quicker and more delirious at our discovery of each other after Ramadhin's death, almost knowing we could not have come together without it.

Then there was the story of Ramadhin's girl.

Her name was Heather Cave. And whatever was still unformed in her at the age of fourteen, he loved. It was as if he could see every possibility, though he must have also loved what she was at that moment, the way we might adore a puppy, a yearling, a beautiful boy who is not yet sexual. He would go to the Cave family's flat in the city to coach her in geometry and algebra. They sat at a kitchen table. If it was sunny they would sometimes have a tutorial in the fenced garden that bordered the building. And during their last half-hour, as a little informal gift, he got her to speak of other things. He was surprised at her harsh judgements of her parents, the teachers she was bored by, and some 'friends' who had tried to seduce her. Ramadhin had sat there stunned. She was young but not naïve. In many ways, she was probably more worldly than he. And what was he? A too-innocent thirty-year-old, in the cocoon of that small immigrant community in London. He was not active or knowledgeable about the world around him. He was supply teaching as well as tutoring. He read a good deal of geography and history. He kept in touch with Mr Fonseka, who was in the north – there was supposedly a rarefied correspondence between them, according to his sister. So he listened to the Cave girl across the table, imagined the various spokes of her nature. Then went home.

Why didn't he break the spell of that high-flown correspond-ence with Fonseka by mentioning her? But he could never have done that. Fonseka surely would have known how to sway him away from her. Although how much of a realist was *he* about teenage character that can be brutal beneath the veneer? No, it would have been better for him to have confided in Cassius. Or me.

On Wednesdays and Fridays he went to the Cave flat. On Fridays the girl was clearly impatient, as she would be leaving to join her friends when the tutorial was over. Then one Friday he found her in tears. She began talking, not wanting him to leave but to help her with her life. She was fourteen and all she wished for was a boy named Rajiva, someone Ramadhin had met one night in her company. A dubious one, he had thought. But now Ramadhin was forced to listen to all the boy's qualities and what seemed a caustic and too-casual passion between them. She talked and Ramadhin listened. There had been a sneering dismissal of her by the boy in the company of his friends, and she as a result felt abandoned. She wanted Ramadhin to go to the boy and say something, somehow represent her; he could, she knew, talk well – and that would perhaps bring Rajiva back to her.

This was the first thing she had ever asked him to do.

She knew where Rajiva would be, she said. The Coax Bar. She would not, could not, go herself. Rajiva would be with his friends, and now they were ignoring her.

So Ramadhin went in search of the boy, to persuade him to come back to Heather. He entered that strip of the city – somewhere he would never have gone – walking there in his long black winter coat, scarfless, against the English weather.

* * *

161

He enters the Coax Bar on his knight's mission. The place is turbulent – music, loud conversation, and smoke. He goes in, a plump, asthmatic Asian, looking for another Asian, for Rajiva is also from the East, or at least his parents are. But one generation later has a lot more confidence. Ramadhin sees Rajiva in the midst of his friends. He gets close and attempts to explain why he is there, why he is speaking to him. There are many conversations taking place as he tries to persuade Rajiva to accompany him back to the flat where Heather is waiting. Rajiva laughs and turns away, and Ramadhin pulls the boy's left shoulder towards him and a knife comes out naked. The blade doesn't touch him. It touches just his black coat above the heart. The heart Ramadhin has protected all his life. There is only the slightest pressure from the boy's knife, its force no more than the pushing or the pulling off of a button. But Ramadhin stands there shaking in this loud surrounding. He tries not to inhale the smoke. The boy, Rajiva – how old is he, sixteen? seventeen? – comes closer, with those dark brown eyes, and inserts the knife into the pocket of Ramadhin's black coat. It is as intimate as if he had slid it into him.

'You can give that to her,' Rajiva says. It is a dangerous yet formal gesture. What does it mean? What is Rajiva saying?

An unstoppable shudder in Ramadhin's heart. There is a burst of laughter and the 'lover' turns away and, with the swarm of his friends, moves on. Ramadhin goes out of the bar into the night air, and begins to walk to Heather's flat to tell her of his failure. 'Besides,' he will add on his return, 'he is not good for you.' He is suddenly exhausted. He waves to a taxi and climbs in. He will say . . . he will tell her . . . he will

162

not speak of the great weight he feels against his heart . . . He doesn't hear the driver's question the first few times, coming from the front of the cab. His head bows down.

He pays the taxi driver. He presses the bell to her flat, waits, then turns and walks away. He passes the garden where they have had the tutorial once or twice when it was sunny. His heart still leaping, as if it cannot slow or even pause. He unlatches the gate and goes into that green darkness.

I met the girl Heather Cave. It was a few years after Ramadhin's death, and was in some way the last thing I did for Massi and her parents. The girl was living and working in Bromley, not far from where I had gone to school. I met her at Tidy Hair, where she worked, and took her to lunch. It had been necessary to invent some story in order to meet her.

At first she said she could hardly remember him. But as we continued talking, some of the specific details she recalled were surprising. Though she did not really wish to go much further than the official, but still incomplete, evidence of his death. We spent an hour together, and then we went back into our own lives. She was no demon, no fool. I suspect she had not 'evolved', as Ramadhin had wished her to, but Heather Cave had settled into a life that she herself had chosen. She had a young authority within it. And she was careful, and cautious with my emotions. When I first brought up the name of my friend, she diverted me easily with some questions into talking about him myself. I proceeded to tell her about our journey by ship. So that by the time I asked her again, she knew the intimacy of our relationship and painted a more generous version of him as her tutor than she might have presented to a person who had not known him.

'What did he look like in those days?'

She described his familiar largeness, the languid walk, even that quick smile he would give out, just once, as he was leaving you. How strange, I thought, that it was only once, for such an affectionate man. But Ramadhin would always leave you with that very genuine smile, so it would be the last thing you saw of him.

'Was he always shy?' she added after a moment.

'He was . . . careful. He had a weak heart he had to protect. It was why his mother loved him so much. She did not expect a long life for him.'

'I see.' She looked down. 'What happened in the bar . . . what I heard was, it was only noise, there was nothing violent. Rajiva's not like that. I don't see him any more, but he wasn't like that.'

There was so little to hold on to in our conversation. I was clutching wisps of air. The Ramadhin I fully needed to understand in order to bury was not catchable. Besides, how could that fourteen-year-old have comprehended the desire and torment he had felt.

Then she said, 'I know what he wanted. He'd go on about those triangles and maths riddles about a train going thirty miles an hour . . . or a bathtub holding so much water and a man weighing ten stone gets into it. That was the kind of stuff we were learning. But he wanted something else. He wanted to save me. To bring me into *his* life, as if I didn't have my own.'

We keep wanting to save those who are forlorn in this world. It's a male habit, some wish fulfilment. Yet Heather Cave, even in her youth, had known what Ramadhin probably wished for her. And yet, in spite of having asked him to do something for her that night, she had never accused herself of his death. His participation was governed by his own needs.

'He has a sister, doesn't he?'

'Yes,' I said. 'I am married to her.'

'So that's why you came to see me?'

'No. Because he was my closest friend, my *machang*. One of my two essential friends, at one time.'

'I see. I am sorry.' Then she added, 'I remember that smile so well, whenever he left the flat, as I closed the door. It's like when someone says goodbye on the phone and the voice becomes sad. You know that change that happens in a voice?'

When we got up to leave, she came around the table and gave me a hug, as if she knew that all of this was not for Ramadhin's sake, but for mine.

ONE SUMMER NIGHT, IN OUR GARDEN FLAT ON Colliers Water Lane, as I walked back into the living room during a party, I saw Massi, across the room, nudge herself off the wall to dance with someone we both knew well. They danced at arm's length so they could see each other's faces, and her right hand lifted the shoulder strap of her summer dress and shifted it slightly – she was glancing down at it, as he was. And she knew he was.

All our friends were there. Ray Charles was singing, *'But on the other hand, baby.'* I was halfway across the room. And without needing to see anything more, or to hear a word being said, I knew there was some grace between them that we ourselves did not have any more.

Such a small gesture, Massi. But when we are searching for an example of what we no longer have, we see it everywhere. And it was a few years since we ourselves had ridden bareback out of the loss of your brother, something neither of us could deal with on our own.

*   *   *

When Massi and I broke up, it was in truth most devastating to her parents, whereas we both hoped to be calmer in our relationship without the marital role. But, it turned out, we would not see each other any more.

Did the years fall away when I saw her move the strap of a summer dress not more than a quarter-inch, so that I interpreted it as an invitation to that mutual friend? As if it were suddenly essential for him to see that small sunless part of her shoulder. I say this long after the bitterness and accusations and denials and arguments. What was it that made me recognise something in the gesture? I walked into our narrow garden and stood there listening to the night traffic racing past Colliers Water Lane that made me think of the constant noise of the sea, and then all at once of Emily in the darkness of the *Oronsay*, leaning back against the railing with her beau, when she had glanced for a moment at her bare shoulder and then up at the stars, and I remembered the sexual knot beginning to form in me as well. All of eleven years old.

I'll tell you the last time I thought about Ramadhin. I was in Italy and, curious about heraldry, asked a docent in a castle for an explanation of all the crescent moons, their tips facing up. A series of crescent moons and a sword, I was told, meant members of a family had taken part in the Crusades. If only one generation participated, then the crest would have just one crescent moon. And then the guide added, unasked, that having a sun on your crest meant you had a saint in your family. And I thought, *Ramadhin.* Yes. He leapt, all of him, into my thoughts, as a sort of saint. Not a too-official one. A human one. He was the saint of our clandestine family.

Port Said

ON THE FIRST OF SEPTEMBER, 1954, THE *ORONSAY* HAD completed its journey through the Suez Canal, and we watched the city of Port Said approach and slide beside us, the sky dark with sand. We stayed up all night, listening to the street traffic, the chorus of horns and street radios.

Only at dawn did we leave the deck and climbed down several levels into the heat and the prison-like light of the engine room. This had become a habit of ours each morning. Here the men lost so much sweat we'd see them drink tepid water from the emergency fire pails while the turbines around them swivelled, flinging their pistons. Sixteen engineers on the *Oronsay*. Eight for the night shift, eight for the day, nursing the forty-thousand-horsepower steam machines that drove the twin propellers, so we could travel through a calm or a storm-filled sea. If we were there early enough, as the night shift ended, we followed the crew into the sunlight, where they stepped one by one into the open shower stall and then dried themselves in the sea wind, their voices loud in the new silence. It was where our Australian roller skater had stood just an hour earlier.

But now, as we docked in Port Said, all turbines and engines stilled, and there was a different purpose and manner among the crew. Their anonymous work became public. The passage through the Red Sea and the Canal had resulted in desert sands blasting millions of fragments of canary-yellow paint off the sides of the ship, so while we lingered for a day in that Mediterranean port, sailors hung in rope cradles, scraping and repainting the yellow hull, and the Engineers and Electricals worked among the passengers in the hundred-degree heat, securing the ship for the final leg of the voyage. The Wipers blew oil sludge out from the pipes, collecting the black phlegm-like substance into barrels. As soon as the ship was free of the harbour, they hauled those barrels up to the fantail and dumped them over the side.

Meanwhile, sections of the hold were being emptied. A brief afternoon rain continued down three levels into the base of the hold as workers, soaking wet, rolled seven-hundred-pound drums towards the mouth of the waiting crane, and hooked the chain and each drum to an I beam. They grabbed and steered tea chests and carpets of raw rubber towards the opening. Bags of asbestos broke apart in mid-air. It was angry, fraught work. If a person lost his grip on a container, it could fall fifty feet down into the darkness. If someone was killed, the body was rowed back to the harbour and it disappeared there.

Two Violets

BY NOW THE STATUS OF MRS FLAVIA PRINS ON THE *Oronsay* was considerable. She had been a guest at the Captain's Table, and was invited twice onto the bridge for Officers' Tea. But it was the combination of Aunt Flavia with her two friends and their skills at duplicate bridge that gave her power within the A Deck salons.

Violet Coomaraswamy and Violet Grenier, 'the two Violets,' as they were referred to by all, had represented Ceylon in numerous Asian bridge tournaments from Singapore to Bangkok. They were therefore superior to the usually listless card players during the voyage, and these women, not revealing their professional status, cut a swathe with their gambling, searching out a different wispy bachelor every afternoon and making him join them in a couple of rubbers.

The games were in reality a slow interrogation as to the availability of the man, with a possible courtship in mind, as Miss Coomaraswamy, the younger Violet, now happened to be trawling for a husband. And so, though she was in fact the most Machiavellian player of the three, Violet Coomaraswamy pretended modesty at the card tables in the Delilah Lounge, underbidding and faltering when she could have pounced. If she happened once or twice to play a Three No Trump like a genius, she blushed and credited her luck in cards, not, sadly, her luck in love.

I still imagine those three ladies surrounding and ensnaring solitary gentlemen who were out of their depth, not even aware they were in fatal waters. The bangles and brooches tinkled and shimmered as the two Violets and Flavia laid their cards down for the kill, or clutched them shyly to their bosoms. All through the Red Sea there was hope that one middle-aged tea planter would succumb to the charms of the youngest hunter among them. But he proved more gun-shy than they had thought, and during our landfall at Port Said, Violet Coomaraswamy stayed in her cabin and wept.

What I most wished to witness was a card game between my aunt Flavia and my cabinmate, Mr Hastie. He was still despondent about his demotion. He missed his dogs, and he missed the spare time when he could read. I longed for the possibility of a tournament between these two separate worlds, and I wondered whether the Violets might be destroyed by him in a fair game – in the Delilah Lounge, or in our cabin at midnight, or perhaps best of all, on neutral ground, deep within the hold, on an unfolded card table, under a naked bulb.

Two Hearts

MR HASTIE'S LOSS OF HIS JOB AS HEAD KENNEL KEEPER
meant the nightly card games did not take place as often as
they used to. First of all, Mr Invernio's rise in authority meant
there was more squabbling between the two friends. And Mr
Hastie, now assigned to chipping paint in bright sunlight, did
not have the same energy he had when simply overseeing dogs
and reading mystical works. In the past the two had shared a
breakfast at the kennels – usually a whisky and then some form
of porridge, which they ate from a washed-out dog bowl. Now
they barely saw each other. But sometimes a late game of bridge
would still take place, and I'd watch the four of them until I
fell asleep, only to be woken by Mr Babstock who was a shouter
whenever he lost a hand. He and Tolroy, on a night break from
being wireless operators, would come to these games exhausted.
Only Invernio, who now had the easiest job, was lively,
clapping his hands at any small victory. With the odour of
dalmatians and terriers rising off him he continued to irritate
Mr Hastie.

By the fantail of the ship there was a yellow stern light.
And during the hottest nights my cabinmate dragged his cot

there and lashed it to the railing in order to sleep under the stars. I realised he had probably been sleeping there on those first few nights out of Colombo. Cassius, Ramadhin and I came upon him on one of our night expeditions and he explained he'd been doing this since going through the Straits of Magellan as a young man, when the ship he was on had been surrounded by icebergs that came in every colour. Hastie was a 'lifer' in the Merchant Navy, travelling to the Americas, the Philippines, the Far East, being altered, he claimed, by the men and the women he met. 'I remember the girls, the silk . . . I don't remember the work at all. I chose tough adventures. Books were only words then.' In the late-night air, Mr Hastie was a nonstop talker. And what he told us, when we visited him by his yellow light on some of those evenings, put an excited fear into our hearts. He had worked for the Dollar Line, which passaged through the canal in Panama – the Pedro Miguel Locks, the Miraflores Locks, the Galliard Cut. That, he said, was the realm of romance! He described the man-made excavations, and the portal cities at each end of the canal, and then Balboa, where he was seduced by a local beauty, got drunk, missed his ship, and married the woman, escaping five days later by signing up on the next Italian vessel.

Mr Hastie spoke in his slow, dry voice, the cigarette hanging from his lips, the words whispered modestly through the smoke. We believed everything he told us. We asked to see a picture of his 'wife', who, he said, continued to follow him from port to port, never giving up, and he promised to 'reveal her image', although he never did. We imagined a great beauty, with blazing eyes, and a horse under her. For when Mr Hastie signed on to his Italian ship out of Balboa, Anabella Figueroa had read his self-blaming but still dismissive letter too late to catch the vessel herself. She gathered two horses and rode without pause and in a fury to the Pedro Miguel Locks and boarded the steamer there as a first-class passenger – in order that she could be served a meal by him in his steward's monkey jacket, and not even acknowledge his surprised face or his servile presence with one word or glance, until that evening when she entered the small cabin he shared with two other crew members, and leapt into his arms. Our dreams were busy that night.

And further tales would follow by the yellow stern light. Because sometime later, on another ship, after he had again admitted his hesitancy about their relationship, my cabinmate was watching a four-day-old moon, when she came silently up to him and knifed him twice through the ribs, missing his heart 'by the width of a communion wafer'. It was only the cold air that kept him conscious. If she had been a larger woman, as opposed to South American petite, he was sure, she would have lifted him over the railings and dropped him overboard. He lay there and bellowed – perhaps his yells were louder because of the stillness of the night. Fortunately, a watchman heard him. Anabella Figueroa was arrested, and jailed for only a week. 'Female despair,' Mr Hastie explained. 'They have a single word for it in the South American criminal code. It is the equivalent of "driving under the influence of hypnotism". Which is what love is, or at least what love *was*, in those days . . .

'There is a madness in women,' he tried to explain to the three of us. 'You have to approach them carefully. They might be quaint and hesitant as wild stags, if you wish to lie with them, go drinking with them. But you *leave* them and it's like plunging down a mine shaft you didn't realise was there in their nature . . . A stabbing is nothing. *Nothing*. I could have survived that. But in Valparaiso she was there again, released from jail. She hunted me down at the Hotel Homann. Luckily I had caught the typhoid, perhaps in the very hospital I was taken to with my knife wounds, and luckily she had an unreasonable fear of the disease – a fortune-teller had told her she might die of it – and she left me for good. So the knifing near to my left heart saved me from a permanent fate with her. I was never to see her again. I said *left* heart, for men have two. Two hearts. Two kidneys. Two ways of life. We are symmetrical creatures. We are balanced in our emotions . . .'

For years I believed all this.

'Anyway, in the hospital, while I fought off the typhoid, a couple of docs taught me to play bridge. And I also began to read. When I was young, books never invaded my spirit. You know what I mean? If I had read this book, *The Upanishads*, when I was twenty, I would not have *received* it. I had a too-busy mind then. But it is a meditation. It helps me now. I suppose I would appreciate her now as well, more easily.'

I was standing with Flavia Prins one afternoon, talking listlessly. Looking down the side of the ship, I saw Mr Hastie straddling a raised anchor, and painting the hull. There were other sailors cradled in rope ladders around him, but I could recognise his bald spot, which I saw whenever I looked down during his card games. He had his shirt off, and his torso was sunburned. I pointed him out to my aunt.

'They say that man is the greatest bridge player on the ship,' I told her. 'He has won championships in places as distant as Panama . . .'

She raised her eyes from him, up to the horizon. 'What is he doing there then, I wonder.'

'He is keeping his ears open,' I said. 'But he plays professionally every night with Mr Babstock, and Mr Tolroy, and Mr Invernio, who is now in charge of the dogs on the ship. All of them are international champions!'

'I wonder . . .' she said, and looked at her nails.

I separated myself from her and went down to a lower deck, where Ramadhin and Cassius were. We watched Mr Hastie work until he happened to glance up, and then we waved to him. He pushed his goggles onto his forehead, recognised us, and waved back. I hoped my guardian had stayed where I had left her, to witness the moment. The three of us continued on, a slight strut to our walk. Mr Hastie would never know how much that gesture of recognition meant to us.

*

IT COULD HAVE BEEN HER GROWING SOCIAL SUCCESS, or perhaps my false testimony after the storm, but Flavia Prins appeared to be less interested in being my guardian. She now wished our meetings to take place briefly, on an open deck, where she ticked off two or three questions like a parole officer.

'Is your cabin pleasant?'

I dragged out a minute of silence. 'Yes, Auntie.'

She gestured me closer, curious about something.

'What do you *do* all day?'

I did not mention my visits to the engine room, or the excitement of witnessing the wet clothes on the Australian when she showered.

'Luckily,' she responded to my silence, 'I was able to sleep through most of the Canal. So very hot . . .'

She was fingering her jewellery again, and I had a sudden thought that I should inform the Baron about my guardian's cabin number.

But the Baron had already left the ship. He had disembarked at Port Said accompanied by the daughter of Hector de Silva. I had heard someone remark that he had been consoling her, so I assumed he had coaxed her to join him in further gentlemanly crimes and fed her cakes as well as good tea in the privacy of his room. He had been carrying a flat valise that may have contained valuable papers and even perhaps the portrait of Miss de Silva herself, which I knew he had in his possession. He gave me a farewell nod from the top of the gangplank and Cassius nudged me – I had told him of my participation in the robberies, enlarging the significance of my role. The de Silva heiress moved beside him in an envelope of silence. That may have been grief. Or was she already hypnotised by the charms of the Baron?

We ourselves did not go ashore at Port Said. We stayed to witness the Gully Gully man, and watched from the *Oronsay* railing as he arrived by canoe and began pulling chickens from his sleeves, his trousers, and out from under his hat. He sneezed, pulled a canary from his nose, and released it into the harbour air. The canoe rocked in the wash below us while he leapt up and down in pain, as a rooster revealed its combed head out the front of his trousers. Then we were treated to snakes falling out of his sleeves. They curled into two perfect circles at his feet, undisturbed as coins rained down into the canoe.

We left Port Said early the next morning. A pilot rode out in a launch, came on board, and guided us out of the harbour. In his unconcerned manner he was similar to the man who had led us into the Canal with whistles and yells. I imagined them as twins, or at least brothers. Completing his task, the pilot strolled away from the bridge, his two-rupee sandals snapping at his heels, and climbed down into the launch that had followed us out. The harbour pilots from now on would be more ceremonial. In Marseilles one came on board in a long-sleeved shirt, white trousers, and blancoed shoes. He hardly moved his lips as he whispered instructions to bring the ship into harbour. The pilots I was used to wore shorts and seldom removed their hands from their trouser pockets. Their first request was usually for a cordial and a fresh sandwich. I would miss their air of loafing, the way they appeared like necessary jesters who felt they could stroll safely and behave as they wished for an hour or two

in the court of a foreign king. But now we had entered
European waters.

*

IT WAS IN PORT SAID THAT MR MAZAPPA ALSO LEFT
us. I waited for his return up the gangplank, even after it was
concertinaed and rolled away. Miss Lasqueti was there beside
us as well, but she slipped off silently when the departure bell
began ringing endlessly, like an insistent child. Then the
gangway dislocated itself from the dock.

I have realised only recently that Mr Mazappa and Miss
Lasqueti were young. They must have been in their thirties
that year, when he disappeared from our ship. Max Mazappa
had been the most exuberant member of the Cat's Table until
about the time we left Aden. He had herded all of us around
with a lighthearted rudeness, insisting we be a vocal dinner
table. He was public, even when whispering something
questionable. He had shown us that joy existed in adults too,
though I knew the future would never be as dramatic and
joyous and deceitful as the way he had sketched it and sung
it for Cassius, Ramadhin and me. He was Homeric with his
list of feminine charms, as well as vices, and the best piano rags
and torch songs, illegal acts, betrayals, gunshots by musicians
who defended the honour of their faultless playing, and the
possibility of a whole dance floor yelling the word *'Onions!'*
during the brief pause of a jazz number by Sidney Bechet. And
there always would be men Ever Grasping Your Precious Tits.
What life there was in the diorama he constructed for us.

So we did not, and could not, understand what had invaded him so privately. Something dark seemed to have entered this protégé of Le Grand Bechet. What did I not understand about Mr Mazappa? Had I not sensed accurately the growing friendship between him and Miss Lasqueti? In our turbine-room discussions we'd concocted a great romance – the way they politely excused themselves between courses at dinner and disappeared on deck for a smoke. It would still be light outside, so we could see them leaning over the wooden rail, exchanging whatever wisdoms they knew about the world. Once he covered her bare shoulders with his jacket. 'I thought she was a bluestocking, at first,' he had said of her.

For a day or so after Mazappa left the *Oronsay* there were re-evaluations of him. Why had he needed *two* names, for instance? And the issue was raised again of his having children. (Someone at our table brought up 'The Breastfeeding Conversation'.) So, I began to wonder if these children had already heard the same jokes and advice that he had been giving us. It was also suggested that he was possibly the kind of man who was joyous only when he was free, between *this* and *that* point of land. 'Or maybe he has been married several times,' Miss Lasqueti inserted quietly, 'and when he dies there will be several simultaneous widows.' We hung on to the silence that followed her remark, wondering if he had also proposed to her.

I had expected her to be shattered at Mr Mazappa's departure, and to wear an ashen look at our table. But Miss Lasqueti, as the journey continued, was to become the most enigmatic and surprising one among our companions. We were seeing a sly humour in her remarks, and she came over and comforted us for the loss of Mr Mazappa, saying she also missed him. It was the word 'also' that felt like gold to us. She realised we needed the ongoing mythology of our absent friend, and one afternoon she told us, imitating Mr Mazappa's voice, that his first marriage had indeed ended in a betrayal. He had come home unexpectedly to find his wife with a musician and had confessed to Miss Lasqueti, 'If I'd had a gun, I would have shot him in the pump, but all there was in the room was his ukulele.' She laughed at the anecdote, but we did not.

'I was so fond of his Sicilian manners,' she went on, 'even the way he lit my cigarette, the long reach of his arm, as if igniting a fuse. Some thought he was a predator, but he was a delicate man. The panache was in his choice of words, and in the rhythm of them. I know masks and personas. I am a specialist in them. He was gentler than he seemed.' Hearing such speeches by her we assumed again a passion between the two. Surely they were soulmates, the way she spoke of him, in spite of, or even because of, the line about his 'simultaneous widows'. Perhaps they would continue to communicate via the ship's telegraph service, and I made a note to ask Mr Tolroy about that. Besides, from Port Said to London was really not *that* far.

Then there was no more talk of Mr Mazappa. Even from her. She kept to herself. Most afternoons I caught a glimpse of her in the shadows of B Deck, in a deckchair. She always had in her possession a copy of *The Magic Mountain*, but no one ever saw her reading it. Miss Lasqueti consumed mostly crime thrillers, which constantly seemed to disappoint her. I suspect that for her the world was more accidental than any book's plot. Twice I saw her so irritated by a mystery that she half rose from the shadow of her chair and flung the paperback over the railing into the sea.

SUNIL, THE HYDERABAD MIND, WHO WAS PART OF THE Jankla Troupe, was by now often to be seen with Emily. I suppose it was his more adult self that fascinated and then tempted my cousin. I could always recognise Sunil from a distance – his thinness, his acrobatic walk. Watching them I'd see his hand move up her arm and disappear into her sleeve, holding her in a controlling way, all the time speaking about the intricacies of a world she must have desired.

But about the time our ship slid alongside Port Said, they did not seem at ease in each other's company. He'd be talking to her as they walked, that lean, strong arm of his gesturing to convince her of something, and then, falsely, he'd try to make her laugh when he saw her lack of interest. A boy of eleven, like any experienced dog, can read the gestures of those around him, can see the power in a relation-ship drift back and forth. The only power Emily had was her beauty, her youth, I suppose, and perhaps something she was not even aware of having in her possession. And he was trying to capture these with arguments or, if that failed, a quick juggling of nearby objects or a one-armed handstand.

Even if Emily had not been with him I would have been curious about him.

I POSITIONED MYSELF AT AN EQUAL DISTANCE FROM THREE tables in the dining room. There was the very tall couple with a small child at one; at the other were women whispering, and somewhere else were two stern men. My head was down, I was pretending to read. I listened. I imagined my ears pointing towards the couple with the child. The woman was telling the man about the pains in her chest. Then she asked him how he had slept. And he answered, 'I have no idea.' At the second table one of the whispering women said, 'So I asked him, "How can it be an aphrodisiac *and* a laxative?" And he said, "Well, it's all in the timing." ' At the third table, nothing was going on. I listened again to the tall couple with the baby, a doctor and his wife. He was listing some powders she could take.

Wherever I was I did this, since Miss Lasqueti had said, 'You must keep your ears and eyes open. It's an education out there.' And I continued filling my old St Thomas' College examination booklet with the things I heard.

'Trust me – you can swallow strychnine as long as you don't chew it.'

'Jasper Maskelyne, the conjurer, set up all the "bullshit" work in the desert during the war. He actually became a magician when the war was over.'

'It is absolutely prohibited to throw anything over the ship's side, Madame.'

'He's one of the sexual predators on the ship. We call him "The Turnstile".'

'We can't get the key from Giggs . . .' 'We'll have to get it off Perera, then.' 'But who is Perera?'

THOSE AT THE CAT'S TABLE CONTINUED TO REMAIN despondent over the departure of Mr Mazappa, and it was for this reason that Mr Daniels organised an informal dinner for its members, as well as a few extra guests. I was to invite Emily, who asked if she could bring along her friend Asuntha. More and more Emily appeared to be taking the deaf girl under her wing. The ayurvedic, at loose ends since the death of Hector de Silva, was also invited. He and Mr Daniels were often seen walking the decks in animated conversation.

We all gathered in the turbine room, and soon we were climbing, one by one, down the metal ladder into the darkness. Only Ramadhin and Cassius and I, as well as the ayurvedic, had taken this journey to the 'garden', but the rest of the group had no idea where they were going and were murmuring to themselves. When we hit the bottom level, Mr Daniels once again sped away into the hollow and mysterious world of the hold. There was some contained laughter as we passed the mural depicting the naked women. By now Cassius had got to know it well. One day, he had managed somehow to get into the hold alone, pushed a crate in front of the mural, and climbed up onto it so he was level with those vast bodies. All afternoon, he stood there, like that, in the semi-darkness.

Mr Daniels ushered us on, and turning a corner, we saw in front of us his garden and a table covered with food. All the murmuring stopped. There was even music somewhere. Miss Quinn-Cardiff's gramophone had been borrowed once more, this time from the watersiders who worked in another section of the hold, so Emily began selecting various 78s from the pile of records. We were told some of them had been left for us by Mr Mazappa. Some guests walked on the ordered paths, alongside green fronds, the ayurvedic explaining – as if in secret, which was the way he always spoke – that oxalic acid from the star fruit was used to polish brass objects in temples. Emily, longing to dance, took the silent Asuntha in her arms, and swaying to the music, moved down a narrow path in her yellow dress, as if a star herself.

When I think of all our meals on the *Oronsay*, the first image is never of the formal dining room, where we had been placed so far away from the Captain, in the most unfavourable location, but of that lit rectangle somewhere in the bowels of the ship. We were handed a tamarind drink that I suspect must have had a finger of alcohol in it. Our host smoked one of his special cigarettes, and I noticed Miss Lasqueti, who was bending down to study some ankle-high plant, lift her head and sniff the air.

'You're a complicated man,' she murmured, coming over to Mr Daniels. 'You could poison a dictator with some of these innocent-looking leaves.' Later, when Mr Daniels described an antibacterial capsicum and a papaya that could be used to break up blood clots after surgery, she put her hand on his sleeve, and added, 'Or Guy's Hospital could use you.' The tailor, Mr Gunesekera, drifting like a ghost among us, nodded in agreement, but he did that for any overheard remark, for it saved him from speaking. He watched as our host, standing now with the ayurvedic, pointed out the Madagascar periwinkles (for diabetes and leukaemia, he announced), and then plucked several Indonesian sour limes, a 'miracle fruit', he called it, which he would be serving shortly.

And so we sat down to eat at a new Cat's Table. The hanging lights swayed above us – somehow that evening there must have been a breeze in the hold, or was it the roll of the sea? Behind us were dark leaves of pencil trees and a black calabash. We had water bowls on the table with cut flowers in them, and across from me was my cousin, her arms resting on the table, her features so eager in the flickering light. On one side of her was Mr Nevil. His giant hands that once dismantled ships reached for a bowl and shook it gently, so its flower rolled in the water under the swaying light of the lamp. He was, as always, at ease in his silence, unconcerned that no one was talking to him. Emily leaned away from him to whisper to the waif. The girl thought for a while and then whispered her own secret into the ear of Emily.

It was a meal none of us rushed. Each of us looked shadowed, abandoned, until we leaned forward to be caught in the light. Each of us moved slowly as if half asleep. The gramophone was rewound, and the Indonesian limes were passed down the table.

'To Mr Mazappa,' Mr Daniels said quietly.

'And to Sunny Meadows,' we answered.

The cavernous hold carried our words, and for a while no one moved. There was just the gramophone's continuing music, the slow breath of its saxophone. A faint mist, set off by a timer somewhere, fell for about ten seconds over the plants and the table, and on our arms and shoulders. None of us protected ourselves from it. The record ended and we heard the repeating scrape of the needle, waiting to be lifted. The two girls in front of me whispered back and forth, and I watched them, listened to them, closely. I focused on my cousin's lipsticked mouth. I could hear this word and that. *Why? When does it happen?* The girl shook her head. I think the girl said, *You could help us.* And Emily, looking down, said nothing for a while, deep in a thought. There was this trench of darkness between one side of the table and the other, and I could see them through it, from the other side. There was laughter somewhere, but I was silent. I noticed Mr Gunesekera also looking straight ahead.

'*He's your father?*' Emily whispered in surprise.

The girl nodded.

Asuntha

SHE SPOKE TO NO ONE ON THE BOAT ABOUT WHAT HER father had done. Just as, when she was a young girl, she would never reveal or admit where he was or what he was doing. Even when he was arrested and sent to his first jail. He had been just a thief then, a man working his trade, on the edge of the law. He had evolved from being a young, confident troublemaker.

He was part Asian, part something else. He was never sure what. The name Niemeyer could have been inherited or stolen or invented. When he was taken away to prison, the wife and child were left with barely a rupee. The wife began to lose her wits, and the child soon found her mother no longer reliable. She would be silent and uncommunicative, or she spat out a fury towards everyone, even to the young daughter. Neighbours tried to help with subsistence, but she turned against all of them. She began harming herself. The girl was just ten years old.

She got a ride with someone and went to Kalutara prison. She was allowed to see her father. They talked, and he told her the name of his sister who lived in the southern province.

Her name was Pacipia. There seemed nothing else the father could do to help. Just this name. Niemeyer was about thirty-six then. His daughter saw him cornered in the prison cell, still lithe, but all his natural gestures were muted. He could not embrace her through the bars. Bars that as a thief he would have slathered himself with oil in order to slip through. Still, he seemed powerful to her, moving back and forth in an efficient silence, like that quiet voice of his that seemed to leap across space and enter you as a whisper.

But it was more difficult to get home. During the journey it was Asuntha's eleventh birthday. She remembered it suddenly, as she was walking the thirty or so miles from Kalutara. Her mother was not at home, or anywhere in the village. She had left a small thing, a present, wrapped in a leaf, a partially beaded bracelet with a brown leather strap. The girl had watched her mother sewing the beads on during the last few, sometimes crazed weeks. She tied it onto her left wrist. When her wrist grew too big for it she would wear it in her hair.

Each night the girl stayed alone in the hut, waiting for her mother's return, barely lighting the lamp, as there was only a quarter-inch of fuel. When night arrived she slept, waking in the later dark, with nothing to do until sunrise. She lay on the pallet and drew a map of the countryside in her mind and planned where she would go the next day to search for her mother. She could be anywhere, hiding in an abandoned village or along some river where trees hung over the fast-moving water. There was the possibility of her mother's slipping down a bank in her distress or failing in a half-hearted attempt to wade across the lagoon. The girl feared all bodies of water; in them you could see the darkness below the surface where it attempted to reach light.

Birdcalls woke her and she left the hut to search for her mother. Neighbours offered to take her into their homes, but at night she always returned to the hut. She had told herself she would keep looking for two more weeks. Then she stayed another week. Eventually she wrote a message on a tablet, which she hung on the wall over her mother's pallet, and walked away from her only home.

She went inland and south, living on whatever fruits and vegetables she could find. But she longed for meat. A few times she begged for food at a house and was given dhal. She did not tell them her story, just that she had been travelling for a week. She passed monks with their held-out bowls, and she passed the coconut estates where the guards at the entrances were brought lunch by someone on a bicycle. She stopped near these sentries and talked to them in order to inhale the meal they were eating openly in front of her. In one village she followed a rice hound along back lanes to the remnants of a meal that had been flung out from a kitchen door. She found a cut-open jak fruit and ate so much of the petal-shaped fruit that she was sick, then overcome with sudden fever. She climbed down into a river and stayed there hanging on to a branch in order to lose the feverish heat in her. She had been travelling for more than eight days when she saw four men carrying a trampoline along the road. She knew where she was. She followed at a distance, till they eventually turned and asked who she was. She said nothing. She loitered but did not lose sight of them, even when they started crossing a field and disappeared over a scrub hill. And so she came upon the tents. She asked for Pacipia and a thin man brought her over to a woman. This was her father's sister.

In certain ways she looked like him. Pacipia too moved like an animal. She was very tall, and appeared tougher than the girl's father in the way she treated the men and women around her. It was a small rural circus she was responsible for, and she held it together with strict rules. She was different with the girl, however. She lifted Asuntha into her arms and walked away from the performers to some thorn trees. She ran her fingers through the girl's hair as she listened to her brother's daughter tell her about meeting the father in jail, the disappearance of the mother, the hunger for meat above all else. Pacipia had met the mother a few times, and she nodded, careful not to let the girl know what she was thinking. Eventually, when she thought it was all right, she put the girl down.

She took Asuntha into each of the tents. The sides were rolled up because of the afternoon heat, and the girl saw the acrobats sleeping in the daylight, facing the wind that came through the open sides, all the way from the coast. In spite of the fact that she had been travelling alone for at least a week, she was still unsure of the place she was now in. But her aunt assumed she was not naturally nervous. She was her father's child, wasn't she? The girl stayed beside Pacipia those first days, hampering her preparations. There were to be some performances during the next few days in the village of Beddegama.

Then the troupe would move on. A new village in the southern province every week. Otherwise her musicians would get enchanted with local girls and leave the troupe. The musicians did not have that much to do, but their fanfares were essential in any circus.

Because of the hindrance of the girl, Pacipia was exercising before the sun came up; anyone who was awake would hear the bounce of the trampoline and in the semi-darkness see Pacipia wheel in mid-air, land on her back or her knees, pivot up once more, further into darkness. By the time the sun rose she was covered in sweat and walking to a farmer's well, pulling up the roped bucket to pour water over herself again and again. There was always that singular pleasure at a well. She walked back in her drenched costume, which would dry in the sunlight, to the tent where the girl would be waking. What independence Pacipia owned had, it seemed, disappeared. She was never married, had no children, but now there was this girl she was responsible for until her brother returned.

*

THERE IS A STORY, ALWAYS AHEAD OF YOU. BARELY existing. Only gradually do you attach yourself to it and feed it. You discover the carapace that will contain and test your character. You find in this way the path of your life. And so, within a few weeks, the girl Asuntha could be found in mid-air, held by an outstretched arm, then thrown towards the grip of another, swinging down simultaneously from another tree. She had her father's strong, light bones, and she had beneath her

196

first fears a self-sufficient nature. She would have to loosen that away from herself in order to allow trust. Pacipia would help. Pacipia too had been full of self-sufficiency once, one of those seemingly stunned-looking children who hold an anger in them; it had scared her parents and the friends of her parents. But acrobats always needed to trust the company around them.

The circus performed along any stretch of country road that was bordered by trees. Villagers brought mats and sat on the tarmac in the late afternoon when it was no longer too hot but before the shadows lengthened to confuse the performers' sight. Then the sound of a fanfare emerged, some of it out of the depths of the forest, some more magically from the high branches of the trees where the trumpeter was. And a man seemingly on fire, his face painted like a bird's, swept down on a rope, skimming the spectators' heads, smoke trailing behind him, catching another rope and swinging this way farther and farther along the stretch of audience-covered road. There were harp sounds and whistles coming off him until the painted man disappeared into a tree and was never seen again.

Then the rest of them came out, in stained and ragged colours, and for the next hour leapt from trees into the empty air and were caught in the arms of others, who seemed to fall from even greater heights. A man covered in flour fell into the central trampoline and rose out of the dust he left behind. Men walked across tightropes stretched from tree to tree, carrying brimming buckets of water, slipping in mid-air and hanging on with just one arm, releasing the contents into the crowd. Sometimes it was water, sometimes it was ants. Each time a man stepped out onto the tightrope, the drummer warned of the danger and the difficulty, and the trumpet shrieked and laughed with the crowd. Eventually the men on the tightrope fell to earth. They curled their bodies when they hit the tarmac, and stood. They were the only ones standing until the people in the crowd got to their feet. It was over, save for one acrobat still up there, still yelling for help, hanging from a rope by one foot.

At first Asuntha would be caught only by Pacipia. But this was not trust. It came from the belief that if this relative would not pluck her out of the air into safety, then she might as well lose her life in the fall to earth. The greater test came when Pacipia stepped away from Asuntha, who was on a high branch, and ordered her to throw herself to another. Knowing fear would grow by thinking and waiting, Asuntha overcame it instantly. There was in fact hardly time for the catcher to move forward.

And so the girl entered into that carapace which had been waiting for her. She was now a member of the seven-person circus that traversed the provinces of the south coast, living in one of four tents, and warned always by Pacipia, who was wary of the adulterous musicians. One day, in mid-performance, while she was in the trees, she saw her father among the sparse audience, and she swung down one-handed to his level and embraced him, and did not leave his side during the rest of the show. He stayed a few days. To be truthful, having nothing to do, he was too restless for Asuntha's and Pacipia's comfort. He quickly realised his daughter was in the most secure place she could be. She would have her own life in this circus, as opposed to a life lived with him.

She had not even thought of leaving with him. And from then on, in the various meetings between father and daughter, it was as if she were the adult watching him as he went further into deepening levels of crime. He visited her once when he was in the heaven-like clutch of addiction, and Asuntha ignored him, just watched him making friends with the acrobat Sunil, the one who wore the painted face of a bird, watched him laughing with the young man, trying to charm him with that voice.

The country was full of stories about Niemeyer during the three years when she rarely saw him – he had become popular as a criminal, almost loved. There was a gang around him, some of whom were killers who haunted and slipped in and out of the political world. He continued to wear that foreign name like a badge, or an insult to the establishment. It was a ridiculous heritage claimed by the man, taken from some possibly distant European ancestor, possibly not, so the name was mocked, insisted on by this 'heir'. Only now and then did Asuntha wish for his presence as a comfort. She had her own dangers. As an acrobat she had broken her nose once, then a wrist, the one that still wore her mother's last gift to her, made of leather and beads.

Then, when she was seventeen, and had grown into all the skill and confidence she needed, she had a bad fall. They were rehearsing for a pretended accident. She leapt from a high branch, kicked herself outward off a tree trunk and missed her aimed-for catcher, fell to the road, and the side of her head glanced against a mile-marker stone. When she came back into consciousness she could not hear what Pacipia was urgently saying to her. She kept nodding and nodding in spite of the pain, pretending to understand what was being asked. The fear that had been absent now was there. So she was of no more use to the six other performers who had become her family. A month afterwards, still without any hearing, she slipped away from her chosen world.

When the circus troupe realised she was not returning, Sunil, who had caught her that very first time when she had to trust someone other than Pacipia, and who had also reached out frantic to catch her during her last fall, was sent by Pacipia to look for her. He entered Colombo and disappeared. Pacipia did not hear from him again.

Sunil was at Niemeyer's pre-trial hearing when he saw Asuntha in the packed gallery of the Colombo courthouse. When it was over he followed her at a distance along a narrow street that had sloping parapets and into a lane that became a street of goldsmiths. Chekku Street. It was like an exuberant medieval lane. She kept on walking, and then, somewhere on Messenger Street, she disappeared. Sunil stood very still. He knew that even if he could not see her, she could see him. She was always quick to be aware of what was taking place around her – and since her fear had returned, that skill would be even stronger. Besides, he was lost now. He had lived in the southern province most of his life; he really did not know the city. A strong hand grabbed his arm. She pulled him into a room the size of a carpet. He didn't speak. He knew her deafness embarrassed her. He sat down and was still.

She spoke with difficulty, with her already slurring words. She appeared to be in a state of worthlessness, her talent no longer in her. He stayed in her room all evening, not letting her out of his sight, and the next morning he took her, as had been planned, to the prison where her father was being held. He waited outside when they let her in to see him.

Her father leaned forward, and spoke a name. *'Oronsay,'* he said. 'Sunil and others will be on the same ship, to look after me.' The vessel was going to England and they would help him escape. Then he put his face almost between the bars and continued speaking to her.

Outside the prison, she saw the slim figure of Sunil waiting for her. She came up to him, held the back of his neck and spoke into his ear, told him what she felt she had to do, that her life was no longer for herself, but for her father.

The Mediterranean

RAMADHIN POSITIONED HIMSELF IN THE SHADOWS.

Cassius and I were crouched in a lifeboat that hung in the air. And on deck below us, Emily was whispering to the man named Sunil. We had guessed correctly where they might be, and could hear each word, their whispers magnified within the shell of the lifeboat. Any sound they made filled our darkness, while we crouched there in the claustrophobic heat.

'No, not here.'

'Here,' he said.

Some rustling.

'Then let—'

'Your mouth. So sweet,' he was saying.

'Yes. The milk.'

'Milk?'

'I ate an artichoke during dinner. If you eat an artichoke and then drink milk, the milk tastes sweet . . . Even if there is wine, I ask for milk. If I have eaten an artichoke.'

We did not understand what they were talking about. Perhaps the conversation was in a special code. There was a long silence. Then a laugh.

'I must go back soon . . .' Sunil said.

Whatever was occurring was not understood by us. Cassius leaned over to me and whispered, 'Where is the artichoke?'

I heard the strike of a match, and soon could smell her cigarette smoke. Player's Navy Cut.

Suddenly, as if they were now strangers, a more cautious conversation started between them. It was confusing. The artichoke dialogue had left us in a different place. Now it was talk about schedules, how often the night watchman patrolled the Promenade Deck, the hour the prisoner had his meals, and when he was given his walks. 'There's something I want you to do,' Sunil was saying, and then they were whispering quietly.

'Can he even do such a thing?' Emily's voice was suddenly clear in the darkness. She sounded scared.

'He knows when the guards will be most relaxed, or tired. But he's still weak from the beating.'

'What beating? When did that happen?'

'After the cyclone.'

We remembered then how the prisoner had missed some of his night walks shortly before Aden.

'They must have suspected something.'

Suspected what?

It was as if Cassius and I could hear each other thinking in the dark, the slow machinery of our young brains attempting to cope with this brusque information.

'You must make sure he will meet you here. Tell us when. We'll be ready.'

She was silent.

'He will be eager for you.' He said this and laughed. 'You must not dissuade him.'

I thought I heard him mention Mr Daniels's name, but then he began talking about a man named Perera, and after a while I could barely keep my eyes open. When they left I wanted to sleep where I was, but Cassius shook me and we climbed out of the lifeboat.

Mr Giggs

THE PRESENCE OF AN ENGLISH OFFICIAL ON BOARD THE
Oronsay had been of little importance to the passengers during
the first part of the journey. We would see him wander the
decks alone and then climb to the narrow terrace in front of
the bridge, where he sat on a canvas chair as if he were the
owner of the vessel. But gradually it became known that Mr
Giggs was a high-level army officer who'd been sent out to
Colombo and – so rumour had it – was twinned with a person
from the Criminal Investigation Department in Colombo, now
travelling undercover. Both were in charge of escorting the
prisoner Niemeyer to face trial in England. It was said the
investigator from Colombo was billeted somewhere in Tourist
Class. We had no idea where the Englishman slept. It was
assumed he had grander quarters.

Mr Daniels announced to the Cat's Table that Mr Giggs
had been seen talking furiously with the guards sometime after
Niemeyer was badly beaten. No one was sure if Giggs was
accusing them of brutality or if he was simply angry that
knowledge of the assault had got out. Or possibly, Miss Lasqueti
argued, Giggs was upset because the attack might have given

the prisoner a way out, a loophole, in his oncoming conviction and punishment.

What I noticed most about the English official were his arms, which had curling ginger hair on them, and which I found difficult to look at. He wore ironed shirts and shorts and calf-length socks, but that red hair was disturbing to me, and when during one of the ship's dances he sought out Emily and began a waltz with her I was outraged in an almost paternal way. Even Mr Daniels, I thought, would be better for my beautiful cousin.

I cornered Miss Lasqueti about Mr Giggs's connection with the prisoner.

'If the prisoner did kill an English judge, it is *very* serious. They won't let him stand trial on the island. They had a hearing, and now the case moves to England. Why do you care? Anyway, this man Giggs is in charge of him, along with an investigator, Mr Perera, to make sure he actually gets there. Niemeyer has got a talent for escaping, supposedly. The first cell he was put in had a heavy wooden door and he actually managed to burn it down and escape, though he was burned in the process. Once he leapt out of a train with a guard handcuffed to him and had to carry the struggling man with him until he found a blacksmith. He's probably not the sweetest chocolate in the box.'

'Why did he kill the judge, Auntie?'

'*Please* do not call me Auntie . . . I don't know for sure. I am trying to find out.'

'Was it a bad judge?'

'I don't know. Are there such things? Let us not assume that.'

I walked away from this brief chat, not sure how to assume a position on what was happening. I saw Miss Lasqueti change direction suddenly and approach Mr Giggs, and I saw that she held his interest and attention with whatever she was saying to him.

At our next meal she told us all what she had learned. The entire ship apparently had been 'traversed' by Giggs and Perera before any of us had even come on board. Accompanying the prisoner also meant overseeing minutiae on every level of the ship. They sealed possible escape routes, removed otherwise innocent objects – a sand bucket for fire drills, a metal pole – that could be turned into weapons. They scrolled down the passenger lists for any known cohorts of the prisoner. They hired guards from the Maldive Islands who would have no connection to anyone in Ceylon. They had spent two days on a comprehensive search of the vessel. Now they were being excessively watchful, and this was the reason for Mr Giggs's observation point in front of the bridge, where he could oversee as much of the activity on board as he wished. He had also told Miss Lasqueti that the seriousness of the crime had governed the level of the accompaniment: Mr Perera was supposedly the very best man from the Colombo CID, and Mr Giggs, though he said so himself, was the best available man from Britain. So it was that they, along with the Maldive Islands guards, watched every step and gesture of the prisoner named Niemeyer.

The Blind Perera

IF GIGGS HAD NOW BECOME THE MOST DISCUSSED AND witnessed man on the *Oronsay*, his partner in attempting to prevent the prisoner's escape was discussed but never in evidence. We never saw Mr Perera, the police officer from Ceylon. Besides, Perera was a common name. All we knew was that he was a 'blind' Perera – from that branch of the family so called because they spelled their name without the letter *i;* for there were Pereras and Pereiras. It was evident the CID had put forward a plainclothes officer, so that if there were any conspirators on board they would not know who else was watching them. So while Giggs strutted about, then parked himself prominently by the bridge, his high-ranking Asian counterpart was invisible. The two of them had boarded the ship and given it a comprehensive search. But by the time we came on board, Mr Perera was simply one of our fellow passengers, anonymous, possibly travelling under another name. Some even began to believe that there might be *two* undercover Pereras.

We spoke often about the mysterious CID man. Who was he? What did he look like? For one whole afternoon Cassius and I followed any strange-looking personality on the boat, watching for abnormal behaviour. 'There are two types of undercover,' Miss Lasqueti explained. 'The social and the private. If you are undercover you make your friends quickly, compulsively. You enter a bar and you get to know every waitress and bartender. You sell your invented character, as quickly as possible. You know everyone's first name. You have to be quick-witted and also think like a criminal. But there are the other undercover workers, who are more devious. Like this Perera, perhaps. He's probably slithering around. It is just that we don't recognise him yet. Giggs is the public side. And Perera – who knows?'

Apparently this invisible and 'blind' Perera was a master of what was later called the 'bump scenario'. This happens when an undercover policeman attaches himself to a criminal, befriending him and simultaneously instilling fear in him by revealing that he, the undercover policeman, is even more manic and dangerous. The gossip was that there had been a case where this Perera, in reality a mild-mannered family man, had walked a suspected gang member into the royal forest in Kandy and made him dig a grave. He insisted it be four feet long and three feet deep, so the body could be folded. There was to be an execution, he said, early the following morning. Assuming from this that Perera was intricately involved with high-level crime, the young gang member revealed his own criminal connections.

This was the kind of work Perera supposedly did on an average day or night for the CID. But we knew none of this back then.

How Old Are You?
What Is Your Name?

WHENEVER WE GOT CLOSE ENOUGH TO SPEAK WITH authorities, we found we had to spend our time answering questions. During the interrogation after the storm, while we shivered from cold more than fear, the Captain kept asking us how old we were. And when we answered he took it in, forgot it, and a minute later asked us again. We assumed he was slow or too speeded up, for he was on to that next question before even listening to our replies. Gradually we realised he was saying the line with a syrup of scorn all over it. That it had within it the invisible question: *How foolish are you?*

We felt we had simply committed a heroic gesture. Weren't the hours we spent spreadeagled in the cyclone equal to that story where the sinner was blinded on the road to Damascus? Later in life it was comforting to discover that heroes such as Shackleton had been expelled from my school, probably for such things. *'How old are you, sir?!'* barked by the headmaster to that too-ambitious and disobedient boy.

It was clear to us the Captain was not fond of his Asian cargo. For several nights he performed what he felt was a rollicking piece of verse written by A. P. Herbert, about growing nationalism in the East, that ended:

And all the crows in all the trees
cried 'Banyan for the Banyanese!'

The Captain was proud of this party piece, and that was probably the time when my distrust of the authority and prestige of all Head Tables began. As well, there was the afternoon with the Baron when my eyes had gone back and forth between the noble bust of Hector de Silva and the seemingly lifeless body asleep on the bed. So that I found myself, shortly after his funeral, approaching the trestle table where the de Silva bust remained, as if forgotten. Cassius and I managed to lift it (he by the ears, me by the nose) and roll it over to the edge of the railing and let the graven image drop overboard to follow the corpse.

Perhaps we had by then outgrown our curiosity about the powerful. We were preferring the gentle Mr Daniels, after all, obsessed with the care of his plants, and the pale figure of Miss Lasqueti, who wore her pigeon jacket replete with cushioned pockets for the transporting of her birds. It would always be strangers like them, at the various Cat's Tables of my life, who would alter me.

The Tailor

THE MOST RESERVED DINER AT OUR TABLE WAS MR Gunesekera, the tailor. He had introduced himself, when he settled among us that first day, by simply handing out his card. *Sew Gunesekera. Prince Street, Kandy.* In this way he announced his profession. During all our meals he remained silent and content. He laughed when the rest of us laughed, so there was never awkward silence from his seat at the table. But whether he understood what was being joked about, I don't know. I suspected not. Still, he was the gracious and courteous one among us, even if he felt we were raucous at times, especially when Mr Mazappa's horse laugh got activated. He'd be the first to pull out a chair for Miss Lasqueti, and simply by reading our gestures would pass the salt, or would fan his mouth to warn us the soup was hot. And he always appeared to be interested in what was being said. But so far, during the whole journey, Mr Gunesekera had not said a word. Even if we spoke to him in Sinhala, he would give a complex shrug and circle his head to excuse his evasion.

He was a slight, thin man. While he ate I'd watch his graceful fingers that could sew up a storm somewhere on Prince Street, where perhaps he was jocular with his chosen company. One evening at dinner, Emily had come over to our table with a livid welt near her eye; she had been hit that afternoon by a badminton racquet. And Mr Gunesekera, his face showing alarm, swivelled in his seat and put out his hand to touch around the swelling with those delicate fingers, as if searching for the cause of it. Emily, suddenly moved by this, put her hand on his shoulder and then held those fingers briefly. It was one of the rare quiet moments at our table.

Mr Nevil later pointed out that there appeared to be a more serious wound across Mr Gunesekera's throat, which he kept covered with the red cotton scarf he always wore. Now and then, if the scarf slipped, we could sometimes see the scar. After this was noticed we did not bother Mr Gunesekera with questions. We never asked him why he was going to England, if it was because of the loss of a relative or for some specific medical treatment regarding his vocal cords. It seemed unlikely he would be going there for a holiday in a condition where he would not or could not communicate with anyone.

EACH MORNING, THE SUN BARELY UP, I LICKED SALT OFF the ship's railings, believing by now that I could distinguish between the taste of the Indian Ocean and the Mediterranean. I dived into the pool and swam frog-like under the surface, tumbled over at the end of a length and returned underwater, testing the limit of my lungs, my two hearts. I witnessed Miss Lasqueti becoming irritated with the thriller she was rushing through, preparing to fling it into whatever sea we were in. And with the others, I drank in the presence of Emily as she sauntered by and talked with us.

'You must never feel unimportant in the scheme of things,' Mr Mazappa told me once. Or it may have been Miss Lasqueti. I am not sure who it was any more, for by the end of our journey their opinions had dovetailed. Looking back, I am no longer certain who gave me what pieces of advice, or befriended us, or deceived us. And some events sank in only much later.

Who was it, for example, who first described to us the Palace of Ship Owners in Genoa? Or is it possibly a memory of my own from later, when as an adult I entered that building and climbed the stone stairs to each new level? Because there is something about the image that I have held on to for all these years, as if it explains how we approach the future, or look back at the past. A person begins on the ground floor of that palace, looking at a few naïve maps of local harbours, the neighbouring coasts; and then, as one climbs higher, from floor to floor, more and more recent maps chart the half-discovered islands, a possible continent. A pianist somewhere on the main level is playing Brahms. You hear it as you ascend, and you even look down into the central well where the music comes from. So there is Brahms, and paintings of vessels lurching newborn out of the docks in some prelude of a merchant's dream where anything could occur – an eventual wealth or a disastrous storm. One of my ancestors owned seven ships that burned between India and Taprobane. He had no wall of maps, but like him, these ship owners could predict nothing of the future. There are no portraits of humans in the paintings that cover the walls on the first few levels. But then, arriving at the fourth level of the Palace of Ship Owners in Genoa, you find a gathering of Madonnas.

At the Cat's Table they were discussing Italian art. Miss Lasqueti, who had lived in Italy for a few years, was speaking. 'The thing with Madonnas is, they have that *look* on their faces – because they *know* He is going to die when young . . . in spite of all the hovering angels surrounding the child with the little spurt of bloodlike flame coming from their heads. Somewhere in the Madonna's given wisdom, she can see the finished map, the end of His life. No matter that the local girl the artist is using cannot attempt that knowledgeable look. Perhaps even the artist cannot portray it. So it is only we, the spectators, who can read that face as someone who knows the future. For what will become of her son is provided by history. The recognition of that woe comes from the viewer.'

I think back, not just to this conversation during a meal on a ship, but also to my teenage evenings in Mill Hill. Massi and Ramadhin and I have quickly eaten a curry dinner at their house and are rushing out to catch the 7.05 train into the city. We have heard of a jazz club. We are sixteen and seventeen. This is the look, the long-distance gaze towards her son, with his unsafe heart, that I would have seen on Ramadhin's mother's face.

LAST NIGHT, MY FIRST DREAM OF MASSI. IT IS YEARS since we separated. I was among alpine houses, the living quarters raised because the ground level was for animals. I have not seen her in a dream, let alone in real life, for a considerable time.

I was hidden when she came out. Her hair was short and dark, which distinguished her from the way she looked when she lived with me. It made her face clearer, there were interesting new angles. She looked healthy. I knew I could have fallen in love with her again. Whereas I could not have fallen in love with her again as she had been in the past, surrounded by a mutual history and a familiar look.

A man came out, helped her up onto a table, and I saw that she was in the beginning of a pregnancy. They heard something and came towards me. I leapt over a hedge, fell on my knees, then started running along a road where there were merchants, blacksmiths and carpenters, all at work. The noise of their tools sounded like weapons. It became music and I realised suddenly that I was not running, it was Massi who was running between the dangerous rhythms of anvils and saw blades. I was disembodied, no longer in the scene, no longer part of her existence. And it was she, newly pregnant, who was in full life racing to escape the dangers. Massi, with her short, dark hair, determined to reach something beyond where she now was.

I must have been taught, or somehow learned early in my life, to break easily away from intimacy. When Massi and I split, no matter what pain there was, I did not fight back. We parted almost too casually. So that, long after my relationship with her ended, but still within the spin and eddy of it, I found myself searching for something to explain or excuse it. I stripped our story down to what I thought was the essential truth. But of course it was only a partial truth. Massi said that sometimes, when things overwhelmed me, there was a trick or a habit I had: I turned myself into something that did not belong anywhere. I trusted nothing I was told, not even what I witnessed.

It was, she said, as if I had grown up believing that everything was perilous. A deceit must have done that. 'So you give your friendship, your intimacy, only to those distant from you.' Then she asked me, Did I still believe that my cousin had been involved in a murder? That if I opened myself up and spoke the truth about what I knew, she would continue to be in danger? 'Your goddamn cautious heart. Who did you love that did this to you?'

'I loved you.'

'What?'

'I said I loved you.'

'I don't think so. Someone damaged you. Tell me what happened when you came to England.'

'I went to school.'

'No, when you *came*. Because something must have happened. I thought you were okay, when I saw you again, after Ramadhin died. But I don't think so. What?'

'I said I loved you.'

'Yeah, *loved*. You're leaving my life, aren't you.'

In this way, valid or not, we burned the few good things remaining between us.

EVERY AFTERNOON, FROM THE TIME WE LEFT PORT SAID, the orchestra, in their usual plum-coloured clothes, played waltzes on the Promenade Deck, and everyone came out to take in the milder sun of the Mediterranean. Mr Giggs walked among us, shaking hands. And there was Mr Gunesekera, with his red scarf around his neck, bowing as he passed. Miss Lasqueti wore her pigeon jacket with the ten cushioned pockets, each housing a *tumbler* or a *jacobin*, their heads staring out while she strode the decks to give them sea air. But there was no Mr Mazappa. His wild, raucous humour was gone. There were only a few excitements, the most important being that the O'Neal Weimaraner was believed to have jumped overboard and swum ashore around the time we left the harbour at Port Said. But we were sure that if the dog had gone overboard, Mr Invernio would have leapt after it into the sea. Still, we were pleased that with the disappearance of this two-time Crufts Dog Show winner, our Captain had yet another problem on his hands. So far it had not proven to be his most successful voyage. One more crisis, Miss Lasqueti said, and this might be his last. In the privacy of our cabin Mr Hastie hinted that the

Weimaraner had been stashed away somewhere by Invernio, since it was clear he was besotted with the creature and did not seem too upset at its disappearance. Mr Hastie said he would not be surprised if Mrs Invernio – if there was a Mrs Invernio – was seen in a few weeks walking the pedigree creature in Battersea Park.

An outdoor concert was given one night on the Promenade Deck, with the sound of the sea filling our ears. It was classical music, something Cassius, Ramadhin and I had never heard about, and because the three of us had grabbed seats in the front row, we were not able to get up and leave, unless we pretended to be overcome by illness. I was not really listening, trying instead to invent a dramatic walk away from my seat while clutching my stomach. But I was hearing now and then something familiar. The sounds were coming from a redheaded woman on the stage, who tossed her hair this way and that, playing her violin by herself while the other musicians were quiet. Something was very familiar about her. Perhaps I had seen her in the pool. A hand from behind me squeezed my shoulder, and I turned around.

'I think she could be your violinist,' Miss Lasqueti whispered into my ear.

I had complained to her about the noises next to my cabin during the afternoons. I looked at the programme that had been left on my seat. Then I looked at the woman pushing her wild hair back whenever she could find a pause in the music. So it was not her face that was familiar, but the notes and squawks that were now beginning to link with the music coming from the others. It was as if they were accidentally joining in on a similar melody. It must have felt to her like a wonderful thing, this, after all those wretched hours in the high temperatures of her cabin.

Crimes Committed (So Far) by the Captain of the ORONSAY

1. *The biting to death of Mr de Silva by an animal.*
2. *The complete lack of safety for children during a dangerous storm.*
3. *Bad and rude language in front of children.*
4. *Unfair dismissal of Mr Hastie, Head Kennel Keeper.*
5. *The recital of a very insulting poem at the end of a dinner ceremony.*
6. *The misplacing of the valuable bronze statue of Mr de Silva.*
7. *The loss of a prize-winning Weimaraner.*

Miss Lasqueti: A Second Portrait

RECENTLY I SAT IN ON A MASTER CLASS GIVEN BY THE filmmaker Luc Dardenne. He spoke of how viewers of his films should not assume they understood everything about the characters. As members of an audience we should never feel ourselves wiser than they; we do not have more knowledge than the characters have about themselves. We should not feel assured or certain about their motives, or look down on them. I believe this. I recognise this as a first principle of art, although I have the suspicion that many would not.

In our first impressions of Miss Lasqueti, she had appeared spinsterish and cautious. The worlds she spoke of had no interest for us. She enthused about brass rubbings and tapestries. But then she had revealed she was responsible for two dozen messenger pigeons billeted somewhere on the ship that she was 'bringing over for a plutocrat', a neighbour of hers in Carmarthenshire. What, we wondered, would a plutocrat want with pigeons? 'Radio silence,' she had said enigmatically. When we heard later of her contacts with Whitehall, the link to the pigeons became clearer. The plutocrat had been a fiction.

But at the time we were more interested in what appeared to be her affection for Mr Mazappa. We were less aware of her growing curiosity about the prisoner and the two officers (one of them still unseen) who were escorting Niemeyer to England. 'The prisoner is just my baggage,' Mr Giggs had remarked to a group of his admirers during dinner, claiming his authoritative role with a false modesty. But what was Miss Lasqueti's 'baggage'? We didn't know. Was it something I might have witnessed during a visit to her cabin earlier in the journey, when she had wanted to discuss my affiliation with the Baron? For if there was ever an unusual moment in my dealings with Miss Lasqueti, it happened one afternoon, when she asked me to come to her cabin at teatime.

So I make my way along an almost forgotten path to that indelible afternoon. I am surprised to find Emily there with her, as if Miss Lasqueti has invited her to join us in order to discuss something serious with me. There is tea and biscuits on the table. Emily and I sit upright on the only chairs in the room, while Miss Lasqueti positions herself at the foot of the bed, leaning forward to talk. The cabin is much larger than mine, full of unusual objects. There is something like a heavy carpet beside her. I am told later that this is a tapestry.

'I was telling Emily that my first name is Perinetta. I believe it is a type of apple, found in the Netherlands.' She murmurs the name to herself again, as if it has not been used enough around her. Then she begins to talk. About herself when she was young, her love of languages, how she got into trouble in the early days, 'until something happened that allowed me to

225

save myself.' When Emily questions her about it, she says, 'I'll tell you about that some other time.'

In retrospect, I see that this description of her past must have been presented in order to ease herself into warning me about my involvement with the Baron, which somehow she had learned about. Beside her, Emily's serious look and constant nodding seem to emphasise that this is most important. But I am hardly listening. I have caught the eye of another face, in a corner of the room. It belongs to a mannequin-like statue with a few of Miss Lasqueti's clothes draped over its bare shoulders and arms. As she continues speaking, I make out a scar on the alabaster belly that looks as if it has been drawn or painted by a recent hand. But it is the face that searches me out, looking openly at me, as if it has no defence. It is like a youthful and less controlled version of Miss Lasqueti, but of course with a wound. The realisation comes to me only now, as I write this, that it may have been a statue of a bodhisattva. I wonder, that secular accepting face . . . Miss Lasqueti's conversation goes on. And if my gaze stayed away from her that afternoon, as she spoke about my connection to the Baron, it was only because I was caught up in that understanding look. Perhaps she had intentionally placed herself on the bed so the figure would beckon to me from behind her.

Later, as we were leaving, she brought me over to what had preoccupied me, and moved the almost transparent piece of clothing that had been covering the cut in the flesh.

'See this? You get over such things in time. You learn to alter your life.'

The sentence meant nothing to me, but I still remember her words. And I saw the realistic wound up close for a moment before the fabric fell back over it. Everything was in plain sight.

Miss Lasqueti had an authority I had not suspected. Looking back, I believe she must have persuaded the Baron to leave the ship at Port Said, warning him that he would be exposed if he remained on board. Then there was a moment so hallucinatory that it could actually have been remembered from a dream, when either Cassius or I had been walking towards her, one night. It was dusk, and whichever one of us it was thought he saw her cleaning, with the edge of her blouse, what looked like a small pistol. This was not a fully believed piece of grit in our portrait of her. As children we were imagining and accepting all kinds of things. We did know she was fond of us. She spent a few afternoons with Cassius, who had become interested in her sketchbook. She was easy to talk to.

There was one further episode that connected in our minds with that possible pistol. On one of the afternoons Cassius spent with Miss Lasqueti, she lent him a fountain pen. He forgot about it completely until he felt it in his trouser pocket after dinner. He came upon her at a table deep in conversation with someone, her handbag on the chair beside her. He leaned over to drop the pen into it without disturbing them, but her bare arm snaked out quickly and she caught his hand that held the pen and took it from him. She had not even turned her head to look at him. 'Thank you, Cassius. I've got it,' she said, and carried on her conversation.

This to us was further evidence.

In spite of all of her opinions, she never appeared judgemental. I think the only person who continually annoyed her was Mr Giggs, and it was because she found him boastful. She said he always spoke of his skill as a marksman, being a good shot. The revelation that Miss Lasqueti was also 'a good shot' was to come much later, with our discovery of a photograph of a young Perinetta Lasqueti, striding away from a perfect target score at the Bisley Trials, laughing with the Polish war hero Juliusz Grusza, who would later represent England in the 50-metre rapid-fire pistol category at the Empire Games. It was in the article on Grusza that Miss Lasqueti's prowess was mentioned, although more space was given to the possible romance between the couple in the picture. She wore a houndstooth jacket and the sunlight shone on her blonde hair, so we now had an alternative vision of the pale spinster who did sketches on the *Oronsay* and now and then threw books over the rail.

It was Ramadhin who had come across the article and picture when we were both living in England. He discovered it in an old copy of the *Illustrated London News*. The two of us had been loafing through the Croydon public library, and we would not have recognised Miss Lasqueti without her name in the cutline. By the time we read it, in the late 1950s, her companion in the photograph, Juliusz Grusza, had become a national celebrity as an Olympic medallist, as well as a force in Whitehall, where Miss Lasqueti supposedly had affiliations.

If Ramadhin and I had known how to contact Cassius we would have made a copy of this pre-Olympic profile and sent it to him.

She had not been, in our eyes, a beautiful woman. If we found her attractive it was because of the various aspects we were discovering in her. She'd been aloof at first only from a guarded shyness. Then it was as if you had come across a box of small foxes at a country fair. The name Lasqueti suggested some European background, but she existed comfortably alongside that specific breed of garden aristocracy among the English.

She certainly had a knowledge of the variety of Englishness. We were, for instance, startled by information she gave out at the Cat's Table during a discussion on hiking, claiming to know certain hikers (one was a second cousin of hers) who, when they went for weekend cross-country walks, wore nothing but their socks and boots, and a haversack over their shoulders. They traversed forests and open fields and forded salmon streams this way. If you ran across them, they ignored you, as if you were invisible, as they assumed they would be to you. Coming to a village at dusk, they would dress on the outskirts, enter an inn, eat a solitary meal, and take a room for the night.

This highly visual piece of information from Miss Lasqueti brought silence to our table. Most passengers were well-read Asia hands who could not quite link their portrait of English life derived from Jane Austen and Agatha Christie with these naked striders. The wayward and uncalled-for anecdote was the first thing to alter Miss Lasqueti from the faded-wallpaper manner she had first presented to us. The hiker story had silenced our table until Mr Mazappa leapt in to return to the inexplicable faces of Madonnas, which she had spoken about earlier in the meal.

'The trouble with all those Madonnas,' he said, 'is that there is a child that needs to be fed and the mothers are putting forth breasts that look like *panino*-shaped bladders. No wonder the babies look like disgruntled adults. I have seen only one image where the child looks as if He is being well fed and intent on the milk He's drinking. It's at La Granja, the summer palace near Segovia, on a very small tapestry, and the Madonna is not looking out into the future. She is watching the Christ child enjoying the breast.'

'You speak as if you know breastfeeding,' someone at the table said to him. 'Do you have children?'

The slightest of pauses, then Mazappa said, 'Yes, of course.'

'I am so glad you like tapestries, Mr Mazappa,' Miss Lasqueti chimed into the new silence that followed this information. Mr Mazappa had said nothing more. Not how many children he had, or their names. 'I wonder who your tapestry maker was? Perhaps it was a woman, of the Mudéjar tradition. That is, if it was done in the fifteenth century. I'll look it up when I'm in London. I worked for a while with a gentleman who collected such things. He had good taste but was tough as nails, though he did teach me to appreciate the fabric arts. It is surprising when you learn such things from men.'

We pocketed these revelations. Who was the gentleman 'tough as nails'? And the second cousin who was the hiker?

Our spinster seemed to have a knowledge not just of pigeon life and sketching.

*

SOME YEARS AGO, IN MY PRESENT LIFE, I RECEIVED A package that had been posted from Whitland in Carmarthenshire and then forwarded to me by my English publisher. It contained several colour photocopies of drawings as well as a letter from Perinetta Lasqueti. The letter had been written after she heard me on a BBC World Service programme on the topic of 'Youth', during which I had briefly mentioned my journey to England on a ship.

I looked at the drawings first. I saw my young lean self, a sketch of Cassius smoking, a beautiful one of Emily wearing a feather-blue beret. The Emily who had since disappeared from my life. Eventually I began recognising other faces such as the Purser, and Mr Nevil, and locations buried deep in my past – the cinema screen at the stern of the ship, the piano in the ballroom with a smudged figure sitting there, sailors at fire drill, this and that. All of them depicting our ship's journey, in 1954, from Colombo to Tilbury.

Whitland,
Carmarthenshire

Dear Michael,
Please excuse the informality, but I knew you, oh years ago, as a boy. The other night I heard you speak

on the radio. And at one point, when you mentioned coming to England on the *Oronsay*, I quickly focused more on what was being said, for I too had been on that ship in 1954. So I kept listening, but I still did not know *who* you were. I could not connect the voice on the radio and the career you have had to who it was on the ship, until you mentioned your nickname, "Mynah". And then I remembered you three boys, especially Cassius, that always watching child. And I remembered Emily.

One afternoon I invited you and Emily to my cabin for tea. I do not suppose you will remember this. Why should you. I was curious about all of you. The Whitehall in me made me curious I suppose. There was not much else going on during the sea journey, apart from you boys constantly getting into trouble . . . But let me continue with my further reason for this letter, apart from sending you a delighted greeting.

It has been a wish of mine for quite some time to get in touch with Emily. I think of her often. For there was something I had wished to say to her during that journey but did not. I had thought that afternoon of simply removing you from the clutches of the Baron. But it was Emily I should have wanted to save. For I had run into her with the Jankla Troupe chap a few times and her relationship with him seemed fraught and dangerous. There was also something I had promised myself to give her that might be useful to her, to help her out, but again I never did. It was hardly apt. It was, shall we say, a future truth, though it was a story from years ago, from my own youth. So I have enclosed in this package that original missive, to be forwarded to your cousin. I did not know Emily well, but she struck me as one who, in spite of her generous self, needed protecting. I would appreciate it if you would send this enclosed package on to her.

I have made copies of some drawings I did on that voyage, perhaps you might enjoy them.

Thank you,
with affection,
Perinetta

It was a two-page letter, but the package she wished me to send on, with Emily's name on it, was thick with pages, slightly yellowed.

I opened it. Writers are shameless. But let me just say, I had not seen Emily for years, and had no clue as to where she was. The last time we had spoken was at her wedding to a man named Desmond, just before they went abroad. I could not even remember to which country. After a brief hesitation, I opened Emily's package and began reading the many pages, written in a small cursive script, as if to underline the privacy and intimacy of the letter. And as I read, I felt that this was about the incident in Miss Lasqueti's past that she had referred to during that afternoon when I had gone to her cabin and found Emily already there. At some point that afternoon,

Emily asked Miss Lasqueti what she'd alluded to, about an earlier moment in her life that had allowed her to save herself. And Miss Lasqueti had said, 'I'll tell you about that some other time.'

I went to Italy in my twenties, for the language. I was *fluid* with languages and I loved Italian best. Someone suggested I apply to the Villa Ortensia for a job. A wealthy American couple, Horace and Rose Johnson, had bought it and were turning it into a great archive of art. They interviewed me twice and then took me on as a translator – of correspondence as well as for research and cataloguing. I'd cycle to work each day, arriving at the villa to work for six hours, then cycle home to a very small room I was renting in the city.

The owners had a son who was seven years old. He was a sweet boy and funny. He liked to watch me arrive on the bicycle, flustered, for I was nearly always late. He'd stand by the stone gate at the end of the villa's long drive that was bordered by cypresses. Each day at 9.00 or just after, I'd be coming down the 400-yard driveway and he'd be waving his arms and then pretend to look at a watch on his small wrist as if he were timing me. I noticed one day he was not the only one watching as I cycled with the long green scarf around my neck and a satchel across my shoulder. Unseen by the boy, one floor up in the building behind him, was a figure in the window, and as I reached the stone gate it disappeared. I could not tell who it was. The next day I saw it again, that distinct ghost, and so I waved up at it. After that I did not see the figure in the window again.

It was busy and difficult work at the institute. Paintings and tapestries and sculptures were arriving at a fast rate, all to be catalogued. There was also the work to be done on the re-invention of the gardens, with Mrs Johnson attempting to transform them back into their original Medici structure. So there was much scurrying about in the halls and terraces, with huge arguments among the gardeners, who had been plucked from estates all over Europe – so we, the translators, rushed in to help communicate the opinions and the irritations.

Horace and Rose Johnson appeared now and then like gods. They strolled into our offices, or were suddenly off to Naples or even the Far East. They came into our work spaces in a very different way from how Clive, their son, would visit us. His entrance was more like a small shell rolling in accidentally, so he'd be there for some time before we were even aware of his presence. Once I came down the staircase in the Grand Rotunda and saw him crouched, brushing the image of a dog in the foliage that was in the lower half of one of the hanging tapestries: *Verdura with Dog*, it was called. From sixteenth-century Flanders. I loved the piece. It warmed up and humanised the great circular hall. Anyway, the boy had got hold of a dog brush and he was brushing very tenderly the coat of the hound. It was a delicate tapestry, a classic of provincial weaving from the Netherlands.

'Be very gentle, Clive,' I said. 'It's valuable.'

'I am,' he said.

It was summer, the boy had no dog of his own in this villa, even with those vast grounds. The parents were away, one of them attempting to get to Khartoum, who knows why, or for what piece of art to be attained. I thought that for the seven-year-old boy the father's absence must have felt like centuries, and I wondered what the surroundings meant to him. A child looks at a vista, or a painting, and he sees something entirely different from what a father sees. The boy saw a dog he did not have. That is all.

Most of the tapestries in the villa were symbolic, the religious ones weighted with icons and parables. The secular ones (of which *Verdura with Dog* was one) were versions of an Earthly Paradise, or about the dangerous or blissful powers of love – depicted usually by hunting scenes. So the dog in the tapestry was in fact a boar-hunting dog. Other tableaux showed a hawk over-powering a dove in a cloudless blue sky – an example of the 'conquering' that comes with love. Love as murder then, or annihilation of the weaker party. But when you saw those works hanging in the Grand Rotunda or in the spacious but cold rooms, you saw their true purpose, which was to bring a garden into a bare stone house. These were tapestries that had been woven in cold attics in some northern country – places that may never have seen a wild boar or a dove or the lush greenery that was found in them. They were beautiful in this new context. They had a dignity. The colours used were humble, background colours, so that a live Florentine beauty who walked a few paces in front of one might appear somehow distinguished by it. Or they would be at times political, to do with ownership or status. They showed the Medici crest – the five red balls of the solar system as well as the blue one added after the Medicis and the French aligned their families.

'This art feels safe, doesn't it?'

Horace and I were in the Capone Room, surrounded by its frescoes, when I realised he was talking directly to me. I had been working there for over a month and he had never acknowledged me. His hand reached out as if to pluck a painted bird from its blue sky.

'But art is never safe. All of this is only one small room in a life.' For a man who supposedly loved art, I felt he was scorning it.

'Come with me.' And he took my elbow carefully, precisely, as if this was one place on the anatomy which was socially acceptable to touch and therefore take part ownership of. He walked me down the hall until we were in the Grand Rotunda, where a sixty-foot tapestry hung. He lifted a corner and held it up so I could look at the underside, where the colours were suddenly brilliant and forceful.

'This is where the power is, you see. Always. The underneath.'

He walked away from the tapestry to the centre of the circular hall, knowing his voice would carry to the perimeter as well as up towards the distant ceiling.

'Probably more than a hundred women worked on this for a year. They fought for the chance to work on it. This thing fed them. This kept them alive in the year 1530, during a Flanders winter. *That* is what gives truth, depth, to this sentimental tableau.'

He waited in silence until I joined him.

'So tell me, Perinetta – it is Perinetta, yes? – who made this? One hundred women with their cold and chapped hands? The man who conceived the scene? What made this was simply a year and a place. It was a time when the only way to identify an artist was by where he came from or where he ended up working. Towns claim half the great art of Europe. Look here – you can see the city mark of Oudenaarde. But of course, one also must consider which of the Medicis bought it for a small nation's fortune, and transported it to Italy, protected by guards and thugs, a thousand miles . . .'

When he talked like that I could have slid with ease into his assured pocket. I was very young the first time he spoke to me. The thing is that men, with the kind of power that comes with money and knowledge, assume the universe. It allows them an easy wisdom. But such people close doors on you. Within such a universe there are codes, rooms you must not enter. In their daily life there is always a cup of blood somewhere. He was aware of that. Horace Johnson knew the kind of animal he was riding. There's a brutality that comes with such knowledge. I didn't know it then. Not that afternoon when he steered me into the Grand Rotunda holding just my elbow and with that same hand lifted the corner of the tapestry, as if it was a servant's skirt, to reveal the bright underside.

I continued living in that world for three seasons, and eventually discovered I did not control any of the paths I thought I had freely chosen. I was unaware of the trapdoors and moats among the rich. I was unaware that a man like Horace treated even those he loved, and those he desired to have in his presence, in the same way that he must have treated his enemies, placing them where there was no chance of retaliation.

In Siena, if you go to the corner of the via del Moro and via Sallustio Bandini and look up, you can read Dante's lines from the *Purgatorio* –

'That one is' he replied 'Provenzan Salvani;
and he is here because he had the ambition
to carry all of Siena in his hands.'

And at the top of the via Vallerozzi where it meets the via Montanini, you discover, cut into the yellow stone –

Wise Savia I was not, even though Sapìa
I was called, and about the misfortunes of others
I was much happier than about my own good luck.

In the great centres of power, you see, competition is based not so much on winning but on stopping your enemy from achieving what he or she really wants.

One Christmas there was a fancy-dress party for the staff, and during it I became suddenly conscious of him circling me, on the half-empty patio. I had arrived as Marcel Proust, my blonde hair hidden and with a slim moustache pasted on, and wearing a cape. Was this what interested him? Did this somehow allow a disguise for his intentions?

He asked if he could get me anything. 'Nothing,' I replied.

'Do you wish to dance across the great cities of Europe?'

I laughed. 'I have my own small cork-lined room,' I said, 'that's probably enough.'

'I see. Then let me paint you. As you are now. Have you been painted before?'

I said I hadn't.

'You could wear that green scarf of yours.'

So it began that way, with me stepping into his consciousness dressed as a man. And I should tell you there is still perhaps his portrait of me in one of the basement vaults of that villa. In that probably still-unfinished portrait I am fully clothed, but post-coital. Though I look demure, as if a gauche little provincial heiress, or the innocent daughter of a friend.

He had of course been the figure in the upper windows watching me cycle to work every morning. He had taken his time searching me out. He continued now in equally slow motion. He interspersed his sketching with endless conversation: his knowledge of tinctures, the choreography of a fresco, the virtues of alabaster. And I, in order to hesitate at the start of this courtship, wore for the first few days my Proust moustache, so that as he greeted me in the studio, he had to embrace and kiss me with the moustache between us. I wore it for some days in his company, forgetting I had it on as we spoke and as I shared stories of my youth with him. I handed all of that information sleepily over to his great curiosity.

He was wise as well as clever. He made me his friend. He was older, and older skills are different, seemingly more gracious perhaps. And I had never had a younger lover to compare him with – or in fact any lover. All occurred with an ebb and flow that was as much conversation as physical revealing. The removal of the green scarf from my neck as I entered the studio, and then one afternoon, when it was a burning August day, he proposed more. One small step. It was perhaps the spell of his words, my education. I discovered how to fold my naked back into him, to go beyond what at first seemed only pain, until even that became a habit of our desire.

Of course I know there's a tradition for this. But to me, then, it was a stunning country, delirious, shocking, full of tastes to be accepted and fulfilled. I'd move around that well-furnished studio afterwards, my skin, my 'tincture', alive to the air that slipped through the open louvres. Wearing just socks, I walked around and touched with the shadow of my hand those earlier demure sketches he had done of me. Often it felt I was all alone in the room, as if he were not there watching and swallowing my presence – something unwrapped for the first time in this room. I was tumbling in that mixture of knowledge and desire. The weight of his arm, the overall weight of him, my sounds against the sound of my lover, how little light was needed to fall on someone's shoulder in a painting to suggest grief or concealment, how close that cup of Caravaggio's rested to the table edge to suggest the tension of falling.

I read Perinetta Lasqueti's letter into the afternoon, catching the flame of another time, the details of the past still ablaze in her memory. A letter so private and intense, in such a different voice from what I was expecting, that it felt it was for an imagined reader.

That was when my spirit grew, in his studio on the via Panicale, where the bells of the city sounded like a recall order during our criminal hour. He looked at me bent over him. He looked over my naked shoulder as I leafed through one of his heavy books of art. Glancing up, I saw our reflected tableau in the mirror, and remembered a similar moment of his son reading on a large sofa of the Capone Room while Horace – as a father this time

– stood behind the boy looking down at him. We were the same, myself and that boy, under the father's control.

That day, on the *Oronsay*, why did I invite you to my cabin along with your young cousin? During the journey I had watched you, and I feared that perhaps you too were being caught in a situation. I recognised the ease of it, and where you were going. But I was not sure. Instead I warned your cousin about the Baron. What I did not fully perceive, or know, that afternoon, was that the truly endangered one was *you*. I had chosen to protect the wrong child. Why did I not see it?

I see my time in Florence through flawed glass, which confuses the pleasure of those days with irony. I would after making love with him in his various ways watch him. The oblong of sunlight coming down the east wall onto his body, all that hair I had not seen on a man, satyr-like, it felt I had co-habited with another species, forest-raised. The green scarf around my English shoulders, as I strolled alongside the smell of the paints and the chestnut smell of our love-making. I thought I was being loved because I was being altered.

Now and then he'd bring out some painting, something Japanese, or a master sketch that he had bought for a fortune. He would take the index finger of my hand, that had loved him intimately a half-hour earlier, and guide it over the outline of a bowl or a bridge or a cat's back – I still remember quite specifically a drawing of a woman's lap, with hands holding on to a struggling cat. Using my finger he traced the lines as if he were creating them, his attempted brush against immortality.

He asked what I did when I was not at work, and made me describe my small room that he would not visit. He was curious about where else I had been, and what else excited me. There was a tentative courtship when I was at school . . . but really I was now running out of things to tell him. Then one afternoon I remembered the tender incident with Clive and the tapestry. I told him of the moment I'd descended the circular staircase in the Grand Rotunda and seen him gently brushing the coat of a dog that was standing in the foliage.

Horace was only half listening to me. And must have thought at first that I was describing a reality, and then he froze and said, 'What dog?'

The rule between us, his rule, had been that there were to be no recognitions and repercussions outside the studio, beyond our hours there. If there were thrown pebbles, they needed to fall through water silently, and without a single enlarging circle. In fact when I was at work I rarely saw him. I shared my teatime with other members of the staff, and took my lunch out onto the second terrace of the garden, so I would have that angry statue of the Colossus brooding over me. I liked to be undisturbed, and if possible read during my spare hour. It was while I was relaxing there one Thursday that I began to hear a frantic breathing, someone nearby attempting to weep or even howl, though all that was able to be expressed was this disturbed repetitive breath. I got to my feet, followed the sound, and found the boy. His father must have punished him. When he saw me, blood rushed into his face and he ran from me as if I had done whatever it was to him. And of course I had. It was my little pre-coital anecdote about him and the dog.

The next afternoon I argued with Horace about his betrayal, howled in the way his son had been unable to. I wasn't breathless. I had prepared my anger and I had come to wound him in any way I could for what he had done to the child. I saw him for what he was, a bully who hid in his courteous power and authority. And I knew he would slip that way through people all his life, learning nothing. When I saw my words would not hurt him, I swept my arm back, then towards him, and he enclosed my fist and swerved it back on to me. The scissors I held pierced the side of my belly with all the force and hate I had flung towards him. He would no doubt claim he had simply diverted the act of anger, craziness. I was bent in two, my head, my hair, almost down to my heels, the scissors still in me. I was silent. I was not moving and most of all refusing to cry. I was just like the boy. Horace tried to pull me up and I clutched my legs. I needed to remain folded, to be a smaller target against him. I suspected there was even a thrill in him for what had happened, and given a different response from me that involved helpless weeping and clinging to him, we would have attempted to make love again, perhaps, for a last time, as if solidifying our completion with the past. He would have known then that it was effectively over. For he would never have allowed himself to be in a position where he had to rely on someone like me again, someone with this clear opinion of him.

'Let me dress it.'

And I imagined him opening up my blouse to look for the blood in its thin pulsing gush on my white belly. I rose slowly and walked out of his studio. I stood in the half-lit hallway. I was sweating. I looked down and pulled the thing out, and as I did the automatically timed light went out around me, and I was even more alone in the darkness. I stood there for an extra minute, expecting something. But he never came out.

For some weeks there had been preparations at the Villa Ortensia for a solstice celebration. Guests from neighbouring cities were expected, as well as artists, critics, family members, the burghers of Florence and all of us who worked in the archives or in the gardens. It was the annual gesture towards the community by him and his wife. It marked the end of the season. During the hot summer months that followed the event, the family would return to America or go travelling again, foraging its way through Russian duchies. Summer heat was not a comfort, even in the high stone rooms of this villa, even in its shadowed gardens.

The event would take place in two days, and I was lying on my bed wondering whether I would turn up or not. Would I hurt him or myself more by going or not going?

I had 'dressed' my wound – such a genteel term – over a small cold-water sink. It was neither a competent nor a wise act and the scar would stay with me for ever. Lovers who knew me afterwards would pause at it and pretend it was either beautiful or not important. And then they would show me theirs – none of them as dramatic as mine.

I walked away, out of that dark hallway of his, onto the via Panicale, and went in search of a chemist. I remember finding one and describing the wound as 'a deep cut'.

'How serious?' he asked.

'Deep,' I said. 'It was an accident.'

He gave me something in the sulphur family, as well as bandages and presses and a liquid antiseptic, something on a par with what had been used in the Crimean War, I suspect, not much better than that. I did not tell him it was for me, although I must have appeared pale, and was probably weaving. I felt uncertain of everything. All that I had was my competent Italian, so I focused on that. And he kept on talking, perhaps wanting to be certain I was all right. I looked down at one point and there was thick blood on my skirt.

I had a long walk home. I stayed in bed most of that evening and the night that followed. I had not applied any of the medicine. I just dropped the packages on the floor. I simply lay on the bed, wanting to think about everything in the dark. What I had just lived through. If there would be a future for me. He was not a part of the argument. This is when I became myself, I suppose.

I could barely move the next day. But I forced myself to get up and stand by the sink that had a long narrow mirror beside it. I pulled apart the blouse and skirt that had become attached to my body, until the wound was revealed. I coated on the unguent the chemist had given me, and then went back to bed, leaving my skin open to the air. I had many dreams. And there were loud discussions with myself. I got up and looked in the mirror in the afternoon light. The bleeding had stopped. I would be all right. I would not die self-condemned. And I would go to the solstice celebration that was a day away. I would not go. I would go.

I arrived late, missing the welcoming speeches intentionally. I was walking slowly, the pain tearing at my side with each step. Still I listened and followed the sound of the chamber music. They were on the petite stage of the Teatrino, the 'little theatre' beyond the second terrace. I had always loved this site, a place where audiences and performers met on an equal footing. A pianist and a cellist were just beyond the gathering, beneath the lit trees. And in the third movement, as it all melded and the music swept through the garden like an ordered wind and carried us within its arms, I was suddenly joyous. I felt contained, as if wearing a coat of music.

I glanced around – at the families, staff, celebrities, who were being given this gift – and then I saw Horace listening to the continuing music. It was as if he were peering at it. Everything else seemed to have disappeared for him. Then I realised he was focused on the cellist, a woman who was joined utterly to the technique and spirit of her art, and I saw there was nothing that could unlock his gaze. I assumed at first she was his sexual prey. But this was, I had to admit, more. Horace might just as easily have been infatuated with the pianist, whose adept fingers raced alongside the cello music and carried it without any gravity, in the act of an engineer as much as a hypnotist. Their art was this shared skill made up of small coils and screws and resin and chords and a learned pace. These rooted this nondescript cellist in black sensually to the earth. And it made me feel deeply content that she was in a realm Horace could never enter, with all his power and his wealth. He could seduce her and hire her and toast her with his wit. He could collect her and swan around her, but he could never reach the place she was in.

At the bottom of the last page she had written years earlier, Miss Lasqueti had added a note:

Where are you, dear Emily? Will you send me your address, or write to me? I wrote this to give to you during our time on the *Oronsay*. Because, as I said, I had become aware that like me in my youth, you were under someone's spell. And I thought I could save you. I'd seen you with Sunil from the Jankla Troupe, and it seemed you were caught up in something dangerous.

But I never gave it to you. I feared . . . I don't know. All these years I have wondered about you. If you got free. I know that I became for a while dark and bitter to myself, till I escaped that circular state. 'Despair young and never look back,' an Irishman said. And this is what I did.

Write to me
Perinetta

TWO YEARS AFTER I RECEIVED THAT CORRESPONDENCE from Miss Lasqueti, I was in British Columbia for a few days, and a phone call came through to my hotel room. It was about one in the morning.

'Michael? It's Emily.'

There was a long pause until I asked her where she was. I was expecting some distant time zone, some European city where it was already morning. But she said she was only a few miles away, on one of the Gulf Islands. It was clearly one a.m. where she was as well. She had, she said, tried several hotels.

'Can you get away? I saw that piece about you in the *Georgia Straight*. Can you come see me?'

'When?'

'Tomorrow?'

I agreed, got the details, and after she hung up I lay there on the tenth floor of the Hotel Vancouver, unable to sleep. 'Get the ferry from Horseshoe Bay to Bowen Island. The two-thirty ferry. I'll meet you there.'

So I did as I was told. I had not seen her for fifteen years.

The Overheard

WE WERE STILL IN THE MEDITERRANEAN, DAYS AWAY from England. The Jankla Troupe was to give an afternoon performance, and during the encore they invited passengers onto their makeshift stage to perform alongside them. One of them was Emily. Soon she was being whirled until she was horizontal, as if about to fly out of the grip of Sunil.

The other volunteers along with Emily were then persuaded to become the top layer of a human pyramid. And once they were up there, this pyramid began to move ponderously across the deck like a many-sleeved creature. As they reached the ship's railing, the acrobats forming the lower part of the pyramid began swaying back and forth, terrifying the volunteers on the top, who began screaming either in fear or with some strange joy they had discovered in themselves. Then this edifice of humans, a few still crying out, turned in a slow wheel and walked back to us. Among the volunteers, only Emily was calm, only she appeared proud of her performance, and when they were let down, it was to Emily that a small award was given. There was much fanfare, and she was hoisted back up onto the shoulders of one of the men in the troupe. Those from the Cat's Table who were there, including Mr Daniels and Mr Gunesekera and the three of us, applauded loudly. Sunil, standing almost casually on the shoulders of another man, approached her and closed a silver bracelet onto her wrist. She winced as the clasp cut into her skin, and there was an awkward moment when her knees almost buckled. I saw a slow line of blood on her arm. Sunil held her steady with one hand, and put the palm of his other hand against her forehead to calm her. They were lowered down and Sunil rubbed some unguent over the cut on her wrist, and Emily bravely held her arm up for us all to see the bracelet, or whatever it was, there on her forearm. This entertainment by the Jankla Troupe took place late in the afternoon, and when it was over, most of the passengers went back to their cabins to rest or prepare for dinner.

It was evening, some hours later. Cassius and I were in the same lifeboat we had been in two nights earlier, when we had learned that Emily was supposed to meet someone here. We sat there in the darkness and heard a hesitant conversation between Emily and a man who had joined her. Then at one point he said his name was Lucius Perera. The undercover Perera, the CID Perera, was talking to and revealing his identity for some reason to my cousin!

'I did not think that you were *you*,' Emily said.

I was running through all the voices I had listened to or overheard during the trip. I was certain I had not heard the man's voice before. The talk sounded casual until Emily asked about the prisoner's condition. Perera responded by impatiently mocking her concern. He kept on, asking if she even knew about the crimes the prisoner had committed.

And we heard Emily leave.

Mr Perera remained behind, right beneath us, pacing up and down. This was a senior officer in the Colombo police force, and we were practically on top of him, so near we could hear his match strike and flare up before it lit his cigarette.

Then Emily came back. 'I am sorry,' she said. Just that. And they started to talk again.

When I first heard Emily speak, she sounded tired, drowsy, in spite of her curiosity about Niemeyer's situation. And when Perera had become impatient she walked away. She did not wish to continue the conversation. I often witnessed this in her – there was a definite barrier not to be crossed with Emily. She was adventurous, polite, but could also close down and turn away from you in an instant. Yet now for some reason she had come back to re-start her conversation with Perera. Was it out of courtesy? Her friendliness felt false to me. I remembered Sunil's earlier remark about the man she was supposed to meet. *'He will be eager for you.'* And then, as if Perera responded to my thoughts, he must have made some advance, or touched her, because she said, 'No. *No.*' She made a small cry.

'This is the bracelet you won today, is it?' he murmured. 'Let me see your hand . . .' His voice was stern, as if searching for information only he was aware of. 'Give me your hand.'

It felt as if we were listening to a radio in the darkness. 'This is . . .' we heard him say. There was a scuffling. Something was happening. No one was saying anything now. I heard a gasp breathed into the wood of our lifeboat, and someone fell. A female voice was whispering.

Cassius and I did not move. I don't know how long we were like that. It was a long time. Until the whispering stopped and it was quiet. We climbed out from the lifeboat. A body was lying there, I could see the man's hands clutching his neck as if at a slash of blood. It must have been Mr Perera. We began walking towards him, but as we did the body shuddered. We froze, then ran into the darkness.

I got to my cabin and sat on the top bunk looking at the door, not knowing what to do. Cassius and I had not spoken, not said a word. We had just run. The only person I would normally have talked with was Emily, and I couldn't talk to her. She must have had a knife, I thought. Perhaps she had left him to get a knife. All my thinking closed down and I kept looking at the door. It opened. And Hastie came in with Invernio and Tolroy and Babstock, and I lay back on the bed pretending to be asleep and listened to them talk quietly and then begin to bid against one another.

*

I SAT ON THE FLOOR OF RAMADHIN'S CABIN WITH Cassius. It was early, and both of us knew we had to talk to Ramadhin about what we had seen, for he was always the calmest, the clearest about what to do. We told him what we had overheard, and about Emily's leaving then coming back, and the scene with Mr Perera, and later seeing the body, hands clutching the cut neck. And our friend sat there, and said nothing, gave no advice. He too was overwhelmed. We sat in silence, as we had after the incident of the dog and Hector de Silva.

Then Ramadhin said, 'Of course you have to talk to her.'

But I had already gone to see Emily. She could barely get to the door to let me in, and in a minute had sat down in a chair and fallen asleep again, her body loose-limbed in front of me. I leaned forward and shook her. She had been smothered all night, she said, by strange dreams; perhaps she had been poisoned by the food at dinner.

'We all ate the same thing,' I said. 'I wasn't poisoned.'

'Can you give me something? Water . . .'

I brought her some, and she just held the glass on her lap.

'You were by the lifeboats, remember?'

'When? Let me sleep, Michael.'

I shook her again.

'Do you remember, you were on the deck last night?'

'I was here, wasn't I?'

'And meeting someone.'

She moved around in her chair.

'I think you did something. Don't you remember? Do you remember Mr Perera?'

She propped herself up with difficulty and looked at me.

'Do we know who he is?'

*   *   *

256

Cassius and I walked to where we had last seen the body of Mr Perera. We knelt down and looked for any traces of blood, but the deck was spotless.

I RETURNED TO MY CABIN AND STAYED THERE ALL DAY. The three of us had decided to keep to ourselves. There was some fruit Mr Hastie kept in a cupboard to have during his card games, and I ate that in order to avoid lunch at the Cat's Table.

I didn't know if what I had seen was what I thought I had seen. There was nobody I could talk to. If I spoke to either Mr Daniels or Miss Lasqueti, it would mean betraying what I knew about what Emily had done. My uncle was a judge, I thought. Perhaps he could save Emily. Or we could save her if we kept quiet. For some of the afternoon I went up and was on C Deck alone; then I came back and looked at my traced map to see how much farther we had to go. At some point I must have slept.

I heard the bell signalling dinner, and a short while later heard Ramadhin's coded knock on my cabin door and opened it. He gestured to me and I went with him and Cassius. There was an alfresco dinner on trestle tables, and we ate where we could be by ourselves. When we walked away, Cassius was carrying a glass of something, full to the brim. 'I think it's Cognac,' he said. Up on the Promenade Deck we found a quiet place, and we stayed there through some bouts of rain, drinking the contents of Cassius's glass as if we were poisoning ourselves.

The horizon was hazy, cut off, and we could see nothing. Then the rain ended. It meant there was a chance the prisoner's night walk would not be cancelled. His appearance would mean a small renewal of order for the three of us. So we stayed on the deserted deck as it got darker.

The night watchman made his rounds, pausing at the railings, looking at the swells alongside the ship, then left. And some time afterwards they brought the prisoner out.

There were only one or two lights on, at this section of the deck, so we were invisible. He stood with the two guards. His hands were still in their manacles, and as he moved forward the chain at his feet slid noisily on the deck behind him. Then he stood without moving, while they attached the heavier deck chain to his neck. They did this in darkness, by feel and habit. We heard him say, very quietly, *'Release it,'* and we had to look more carefully to realise he was holding one guard's neck at a strange angle. The prisoner lowered himself to his feet, bringing the guard down with him, and rolled sideways, so the man could unlock the chain connected to the metal collar around his neck. As soon as it was unclasped, he shook his head free of it.

'Throw down the keys for my feet.' He was now speaking to the other guard. He must have known that each of them had a separate set of keys. Once more he spoke in a quiet voice that gave that powerless man power.

'The key, or I break his neck.'

The other guard did not move and Niemeyer twisted the body and the guard was still, perhaps unconscious. There was a moan. But it was not from the man but from the deaf girl, his daughter, who came out from the shadows. Clouds were beginning to race past the moon, so there was more light reflected on the deck. The horizon had cleared. If the prisoner was hoping to make his escape in darkness, it was not going to happen.

The girl came forward, bent over the stilled guard, and looked at her father and shook her head. Then she spoke to the other guard, in that difficult, unused voice. 'Give him the key. For his feet. Please. He will kill him.' The second guard bent towards Niemeyer with the key, and she and the prisoner did not move while the man struggled with the lock. Then Niemeyer rose, his eyes darting and looking over the railing into the distance. Until that moment he must have been conscious only of his given space, the extent of the tether, but now there was the possibility of escape. His legs were free. Only his hands were chained together, with the padlock in front of him. Then the night watchman came out, saw it all, and blew his whistle. And suddenly everything was in motion, the deck filling with sailors, other guards, and passengers. Niemeyer took hold of the girl and ran, looking for some exit. He stopped at the stern railing. We thought he might leap over, but he turned around and looked back. But no one came close to him. We crept out of our corner. There was no use in hiding, there was no use in not being able to see properly.

For a moment everyone was poised there, with the lights of Naples, or was it Marseilles, in the far distance. Niemeyer moved forward with Asuntha, and as he did the crowd shifted back and a narrow path was created, the people not shouting but saying, as if complaining, 'The girl! Release the girl! Let her go!' But no one dared block the pathway and contain him in the crowd, this manacled barefoot man with his daughter. And in all that time the girl did not scream. Her face remained the one unemotional thing amid the rage that was building, just her two large eyes watching everything as Niemeyer loped through this tunnel he had been allowed. *'Release the girl!'*

Then someone fired a pistol and lights went on everywhere, all over the deck, on the bridge above us, and in the windows of the dining room, and this unexpected abundant light spilled off the deck like liquid into the sea. We saw the ashen girl clearly. Someone yelled – it was precisely enunciated, *'Do not give him the last key.'* And I heard Ramadhin near me say very quietly, 'Give him the key.' For all at once it was clear the prisoner was a danger to the girl, to everyone, *without* whatever key it was. If the girl's face had no expression, the prisoner's had a wild quality we had not witnessed during those nights when we had watched him walking the deck. Each time he moved, the narrow corridor widened to let him pass. He was contained in this limited freedom, with nowhere to go. Then he paused, held the girl's face close to himself, in his large hands. And began to run again, dragging her through that tunnel of men. Suddenly he leapt onto the railing and hauled the girl up into his arms and stood there as if about to jump off the ship into the dark sea.

A searchlight moved slowly onto the two figures.

There was a growing wind we had been unaware of until

now. I was holding on to Ramadhin, but Cassius had moved closer to Niemeyer and Asuntha, the girl he had always shown concern for, had wished to protect. A few feet in front of me I could see Emily. The voice that had warned everyone about the key had come from Mr Giggs, high above us on the bridge, surrounded by lights. And the pistol he had fired into the air was now aimed at the prisoner and the girl in his arms. He and the Captain beside him were shouting orders to the crew, and the ship shuddered and slowed. We could hear the wash against the hull. Nothing moved. There were only some distant lights marking a coast off the starboard side.

During these moments, with the girl hoisted up into her father's arms, I kept looking back to Mr Giggs on the bridge. It was clear everything that would happen now would be determined by him.

'Get *down*!' he yelled. But Niemeyer refused. He stayed as he was. He looked at the sea below him. The girl looked at nothing. Giggs kept the pistol pointed at the prisoner. There was a gunshot. And as if on a signal, the ship jerked and began moving forward again.

I was turning back to look at Niemeyer, when I saw Emily. Her face was intently watching something on the far side of the deck. I swept my eyes over to that location, and just as I did, I saw Miss Lasqueti fling something out of her hands into the sea. If I had turned even a second later, if I had paused, I would not have seen this.

Niemeyer was very still, as if waiting for the pain. The eighteen-inch chain that held his hands together hung down in front of him. Had the bullet missed him? He looked towards

Giggs, who seemed to be clutching his arm. Had the gun misfired? Giggs's pistol had hit the deck below the bridge and discharged a shot into the darkness. Nearly everyone was watching either Niemeyer and the girl or the bridge. But my eyes stayed with Miss Lasqueti and saw her quick recovery back to innocence, as if just one of the spectators, so that what I had seen felt like a hallucination. The gesture of an arm flinging something, some object, into the sea could have meant nothing. Except that Emily had been watching her too. It could have been one of her half-read books, or it could have been her pistol.

Giggs was gripping his injured arm. And Niemeyer was balanced on the stern railing. Then the prisoner, never letting go of his embrace of the girl with his manacled hands, leapt into the sea.

*

EMILY'S EYES MUST HAVE WATCHED ALL THAT HAD taken place with an awareness of what was occurring. But afterwards she said nothing. In all the comings and goings after that leap to their deaths in the attempted escape, Emily said not a word. During the previous week I'd often witnessed her bend towards Asuntha to talk or to listen to her, and had seen my cousin again and again in the presence of Sunil. But whatever Emily's role had been in that event, it was to exist unspoken, throughout most of our lives. Did I witness something else below the surface of what had happened that night? Was it all part of a boy's fervent imagination? I swung around, looking for Cassius, and then went towards him, but my friend seemed quietened by what had happened and withdrew from me, as if I was a stranger.

This journey was to be an innocent story within the small parameter of my youth, I once told someone. With just three or four children at its centre, on a voyage whose clear map and sure destination would suggest nothing to fear or unravel. For years I barely remembered it.

The Breaker's Yard

I BOARDED THE *QUEEN OF CAPILANO* AT HORSESHOE BAY
at about a quarter to two, and, as the ferry left Vancouver, I
climbed the stairs to the sun deck. I was in a parka and I let
the wind beat the hell out of me as the boat rumbled into a
blue landscape of estuaries and mountains. It was a small ferry
with several rules of warning posted here and there to tell
you what you could and could not do. There was even a sign
disallowing clowns on the boat, apparently the result of some
fracas a few months earlier. The ferry entered the channel, and
I stayed up there being buffeted by the winds, looking towards
Bowen Island. It was a brief trip. After twenty minutes we
docked, and they began letting the foot passengers off. What
would Emily be like now, I wondered. Now and then I had
heard stories about her escapades, for she'd latched on to a
wild group of friends in London while finishing her last two
years of school. We had found ourselves moving in different
worlds, and distant from each other. The last time we'd met
was at her wedding to the man named Desmond, when I had
got drunk at the reception and not stayed long.

I recognised no one as I walked over the sliding metal ramp.

She was not there to meet me. I waited as the cars drove off the ferry. Five minutes passed, and so I started up the road.

There was a woman alone in the small park across the way. She shrugged herself off the tree she was leaning against. I recognised the walk, the gestures, as she came cautiously towards me. Emily smiled.

'Come. The car's over there. Welcome to my neck of the woods. I love that phrase. As if it were part of a body.' She was trying not to be shy. But of course we both were, and we didn't say anything as we walked to her car. I realised she had probably been watching me as I'd stood there on the dock and looked around for her, making sure I was what she might have been expecting.

We drove off quickly, and after going through the town, she slowed the car onto the shoulder and turned off the ignition. She leaned over and kissed me.

'Thank you for coming.'

'One in the morning! You always call people at one in the morning?'

'Always. No. I was trying to get you all day. I tried about ten hotels before I found where you were. Then you must have been out. I was afraid you might be leaving before we could meet up. Are you okay?'

'Yes. Hungry. Surprised by all this.'

'We can eat at home. I've got some lunch for us.'

We went along the road and then veered onto a narrow lane towards the water. We were going downhill, and she turned

266

onto an even narrower track called Wanless Road. It really didn't deserve a name. There were four or five cottages overlooking the sea, and she snuggled the car beside one. It looked like a place of solitude, though the nearest neighbour was twenty yards away. Inside, the cottage felt even smaller, but its deck looked out onto water and infinity.

Emily made sandwiches, opened up two beers, and pointed me towards the one armchair. Then she threw herself onto the sofa. And we began talking immediately, about our lives, her years with her husband in Central America, then South America. His nomadic career as an electronics expert meant their friends changed every few years. Then she had left him. She said the marriage had been a cautious one, and she had stepped out of it, recognising it was 'too cold a building' to live in for the rest of her life. It was some years since the break-up, so she could speak with easy authority about what had happened, sketching with her hands in the air above her the situations they had lived through, the landscapes they had lived in. It was as if my faraway connection to Emily made it possible for her to be open with me. So she drew her life for me, as she spoke. And then she was quiet, and we just watched each other.

I remembered something about Emily at the time of her marriage. The wedding was, as they all seemed to be in those days, a culmination, a clarity of shared purpose. Desmond was good-looking and Emily a catch. There were few other considerations in those days for a successful marriage. Anyway, at some stage before I left the reception I happened to notice her. She was leaning against a door and looking at Desmond.

There was a distance in her gaze, as if what she was doing now was something that had to be done. Then she had quickly slipped back into the spirit of the party. Who would recall those few seconds at the wedding? But that is what I've always thought of when I remembered her marriage – that it was an escape perhaps from disorder, just as in an earlier time she had escaped a tempestuous, uncertain father by being sent to school in another country. So there had been that look in her face. As if she was considering the worthiness of something she had bought or had just been given.

And so I continued to watch Emily, this person who had been for a while some kind of despot of beauty in my youth. Though I knew her also as quiet and cautious, even if she sometimes gave off the air of an adventurer. But the stories of her married life, in their various postings, and the affairs of the heart that had occurred, seemed a familiar version of my cousin, as she had been on the *Oronsay*.

Had she become the adult she was because of what had happened on that journey? I didn't know. I would never know how much it had altered her. I simply thought it over to myself at that moment in Emily's spare cottage on one of the Gulf Islands, where she appeared to be living alone, seeming to hide herself away.

'Do you remember our time on the *Oronsay*, the ship we took?' I finally asked.

We had never spoken about the journey. I'd come to believe she'd buried or genuinely denied the existence of what had happened that night by the lifeboat. As far as I could tell, it seemed to have been for Emily just a three-week journey that led to a vivid life in England. It felt strange how little all of it appeared to mean to her.

'Oh, yes,' she exclaimed, as if prodded and given a name she really ought to have remembered. Then she added, 'You were, I recall, a real *yakka*, a real demon.'

'I was just young,' I said. She squinted at me thoughtfully. I could see she was beginning to approach her memory of it now, glimpsing a few incidents.

'I remember you caused a lot of trouble. Flavia really had her hands full. God, Flavia Prins. I wonder if she is still alive . . .'

'I believe she lives in Germany,' I said.

'Ahhh . . .' She dragged it out. She was thinking deeper into herself.

We stayed in her pine-walled living room till it became dark. Every now and then she turned to watch the ferries trail back and forth between Snug Cove and Horseshoe Bay. They would let free one long moan in mid-channel. By now they were the only lit objects moving in the blue-grey darkness. She said if she woke at six, she'd see the dawn ferry slide along the horizon. I realised this had become Emily's world, the landscape of each of her days and evenings and nights.

'Come. Let's go for a walk,' she said.

And so we began to climb the steep incline of the road we had driven down hours earlier, walking over the scurrying leaves.

'How did you end up here? You haven't said. When did you come to Canada?'

'About three years ago. When the marriage ended I came out here and bought this cottage.'

'Did you ever think of contacting me?'

'Oh Michael, your world . . . my world.'

'Well, now we have met.'

'Yes.'

'So you live alone.'

'You always were inquisitive. Yes, I see someone. What shall I say . . . he's had a difficult life.'

I recalled she always had known troubled, risky people. There had been a long arc to this aspect of her. I thought back to when she had arrived in England to become a boarder at Cheltenham Ladies' College. I'd see her during the holidays, still part of the Sri Lankan community in London, some boyfriend hovering beside her. There was an air of anarchy about her new friends. And one weekend during her last year, she had slipped through the school gates, climbed onto the back of someone's motorcycle, and roared off through the Gloucestershire landscape. In the accident she broke her arm, and as a result of the incident was expelled from the school. So she was then no longer a fully trusted part of that close-knit Asian community. She eventually got away from all that by marrying Desmond. It had been a quick wedding, he had been offered a post abroad, it was waiting for him, and they left soon after. Then, when her marriage finally ended, Emily decided for some sad reason on a sort of exile on this quiet island on the west coast of Canada.

270

It seemed a not quite real life compared with what she and I probably imagined when we were young. I still had memories of us on bicycles being slammed by a monsoon rain, or Emily sitting cross-legged on a bed as she talked about that school in India, and her lean brown arms waving to me during one of our dances. I thought of those moments as I walked beside her now.

'How long are you here, in the West?'

'Just another day,' I said. 'I fly tomorrow.'

'Where? Where to?'

I was embarrassed. 'To Honolulu, actually.'

'*Hon-o-lu-lu!*' She sounded it out wistfully.

'I'm sorry.'

'No it's okay. It's okay. Thank you for coming, Michael.'

I said, 'You helped me once. Do you remember?'

My cousin said nothing. Either she remembered that morning in her cabin or she did not. Either way she was silent, and I left it at that.

'Is there anything I can do for you?' I asked, and she looked over at me with a smile that conceded this was not a life she had expected or chosen.

'Nothing, Michael. You won't make me understand all this. I don't think you can love me into safety.'

We ducked under the cedar branches, returned down the wooden steps, and entered the cottage through the green door. We were both tired, but wanted to stay awake. We went onto her deck.

'Without the ferries, I would be lost. There'd be no time at all . . .'

She was quiet for a moment.

'He died, you know.'

'Who?'

'My father.'

'I'm sorry.'

'I just need to tell someone who knew him . . . who knew what he was like. I was supposed to fly back for his funeral. But I don't even belong there any more. I'm like you.'

'We don't belong anywhere, I guess.'

'Do you remember him? At all?'

'Yes. There was nothing you could do that was right. I remember his temper. But he loved you.'

'I was scared all through my childhood. The last time I saw him was when I left as a teenager . . .'

'I remember you told me your nightmares.'

She began to turn away, as if she wished to think about it by herself now. She was turning but I did not want her to let go of the past. So I tried to talk again about our time on the ship, about what happened near the end of the voyage.

'On the *Oronsay*, do you think you saw yourself in any way in that girl you got close to? The prisoner's daughter. She too was caught up with her father's life.'

'It's possible. But I think I just wanted to help her. You know.'

'That night, when you were beside the lifeboat, with the undercover policeman – Perera – I overheard you. I heard what happened.'

'You did? Why didn't you tell me?'

'I did tell you. I came to you the next morning. You couldn't remember anything. You seemed drugged, half asleep.'

'I was supposed to try and get something from him . . . for them. But I was so disoriented.'

'The man was killed that night. Did you have the knife?'

She was silent.

'There was no one else there.'

We were close to each other, huddled up in our coats. In the darkness I could hear waves on the shore.

'Yes, there was,' she said. 'There was the daughter, Asuntha, and Sunil nearby. I was being protected by them . . .'

'So *they* had the knife? Did they give it to you?'

'I don't know. That's the point. I'm not sure what happened. It's vile, isn't it?' she said. She lifted her chin.

I waited for her to say more.

'I'm cold. Let's go in.'

But once inside, she was apprehensive.

'What did they want you to take from the man who was killed? From Perera?'

She got up from the sofa and went to the fridge, opened it, stood there for a moment, then returned with nothing. It became clear that she was living on her nerves.

'There were apparently only two keys on the ship that could open the padlock on the prisoner's chain. The English soldier, Giggs, had one. Mr Perera had the other. Sunil suspected the man who turned out to be Perera was interested in me, so he asked me to arrange to meet him at the lifeboat. By then, of course, Sunil knew I would do anything for him. I was in his thrall. I was the lure, I suppose.'

'And who was it? I thought no one knew who the undercover man was, as he moved about the ship.'

'It was someone who never spoke to anyone. It was your tailor at the Cat's Table, Gunesekera.'

'But he never spoke. He *couldn't* speak. And I heard a man talking with you by the lifeboat.'

'Somehow Sunil discovered he was the undercover man. He'd come across him talking to the English officer. So he *could* talk.'

I thought I could save you, Miss Lasqueti had written somewhere in her letter to me. *But I had run into Emily with the man from the Jankla Troupe. She was caught up with him, in something fraught and dangerous.*

Over the years, confusing fragments, lost corners of stories, have a clearer meaning when seen in a new light, a different place. I remembered how Mr Nevil spoke of separating the remnants from dismantled steamers in a breaker's yard to give them a new role and purpose. So I found myself no longer with Emily, on Bowen Island, but within those events in the past, trying to recall the afternoon when my cousin was part of a circus troupe's stunt and a bracelet was put on her and broke the skin on her wrist. I was remembering too that silent man who wore the red scarf around his neck, the man we thought of as the tailor, and how we had not seen him at the Cat's Table during the final days of the journey.

'You know what I remember about Mr Gunesekera?' I said. 'I remember how *kind* he was. That day you had the welt by your eye, when you came over to our table – you'd been swiped by a badminton racquet, you said. And he reached out to touch it. Perhaps he could imagine how you might have been hurt, that it wasn't an accident at all, but had been caused by someone,

Sunil perhaps, asking you to do what he wanted. You thought Gunesekera was attracted to you, but perhaps he was just concerned for you.'

'That night by the lifeboat – I can't remember now – I think he made a move towards me, grabbed my hand. He seemed dangerous. And Sunil and Asuntha suddenly came forward . . . Let's stop now. Please, Michael, I can't do this. Okay?'

'Maybe he wasn't attacking you. I think he wanted to look at the cut on your wrist. He must have seen Sunil put that bracelet on you after the pyramid event, breaking the skin, and then rubbing something on it. In fact *he* was the one who was protective of you. And he was killed.'

Emily did not say anything.

'When I couldn't wake you the next morning, I kept shaking you, and you said you felt poisoned. Perhaps they'd taken something from Mr Daniels's garden to drug or confuse you. So you wouldn't remember. There were poisons there, you know.'

'In that beautiful garden?'

Emily had been looking down at her hands. She suddenly shifted and stared at me, as if everything she had believed, every foothold for years, had been a lie. 'I've thought all along I was the one who killed him,' she said quietly. 'Maybe I did.'

'Cassius and I believed you'd killed him,' I said. 'We saw the body. But I don't think you did.'

She leaned forward on the sofa and covered her face with her hands. She remained like that for a moment. I watched her, saying nothing.

'Thank you.'

'But you were helping them escape. And as a result, Niemeyer and the girl died.'

'Perhaps.'

'What do you mean, "perhaps"?'

'Just perhaps.'

I was suddenly angry. 'The girl, Asuntha, she had a whole life ahead of her. She was a *child*.'

'Seventeen. I was seventeen too. We all became adults before we were adults. Do you ever think that?'

'She didn't even scream.'

'She couldn't. She had the key in her mouth. That was where she kept it. After it was taken from Perera. That was what they needed for them to escape.'

*

I WOKE ON THE SOFA BED, THE CURTAINLESS LIVING room full of light. Emily was sitting in the armchair watching me, as if noting what I had become after the passage of years, adjusting her assessment of the disobedient boy who had lived near her for a period of time in his youth. At some point the night before, she had told me she'd read my books, and that whenever she browsed through she spent her time putting two and two together – some fictional incident with the original drama that had happened in her presence, or an episode in a garden that was clearly my uncle's garden beside the High Level Road. We had each changed places. She was no longer the focus of obsessed swains. I was no longer at the Cat's Table. But for me Emily was still the unreachable face.

A writer, I cannot remember who, spoke of a person having 'a confusing grace'. With an uncertainty alongside her warmth, that is how Emily has always been for me. You trusted her but she didn't trust herself. She was 'good', but she was not that way in her own eyes. Those qualities still had not balanced out somehow, or agreed with each other.

She sat there, her hair was pinned up, and she was hugging her knees. Her face in the morning light was beautiful in a more human way. What does that mean? I suppose it means I could read all aspects of her beauty now. She was at ease, her face reflected more of herself. And I understood how the darker aspects were folded within that generosity. They did not negate a closeness. I realise that for most of my life the one I have never been able to let go of is Emily, in spite of our disappearances and separations.

'You have a ferry to catch,' she said.

'Yes.'

'Now you know where I live, come and see me.'

'I will.'

The Key in His Mouth

EMILY DROVE ME DOWN TO THE HARBOUR AND I WALKED onto the ferry with the other passengers. She had said goodbye to me in the car, but didn't get out, though the car stayed there and she must have watched my progress through the glaze of the windscreen that made her invisible to me. I climbed the two flights to the upper deck and looked back at the island, its cottages littering the hill, and by the dock the red car that held her inside. The ferry lurched and we set off. It was cold but I stayed up there on the top deck. A twenty-minute ferry ride that felt like an echo, a small rhyme from the past, as my cousin Emily had been to me during this last day and night.

I once had a friend whose heart 'moved' after a traumatic incident that he refused to recognise. It was only a few years later, while he was being checked out by his doctor for some minor ailment, that this physical shift was discovered. And I wondered then, when he told me this, how many of us have a moved heart that shies away to a different angle, a millimetre or even less from the place where it first existed, some repositioning unknown to us. Emily. Myself. Perhaps even Cassius. How have our emotions glanced off rather than directly faced others ever since, resulting in simple unawareness or in some cases cold-blooded self-sufficiency that is damaging to us? Is this what has left us, still uncertain, at a Cat's Table, looking back, looking back, searching out those we journeyed with or were formed by, even now, at our age?

And then I thought, for the first time in years, about Ramadhin's wayward fibrillating heart, that he was aware of, and took such care of during that voyage, treating himself like someone in an incubator while Cassius and I ran about joyful and dangerous around him. It had been so long since that voyage and since those afternoons with him in Mill Hill. But it was Ramadhin, the unwild one, who did not survive. So what was better for us all – an ignorance, or a cautiousness like his, towards our own hearts?

I was still on the upper deck of the ferry, looking back over the stern towards that green island. Imagining Emily winding her way back to her new home, so far from the place she was born into. A small cabin on a temperate coast, that she shared sometimes with a man. She had journeyed after all these years to another island. But an island can imprison you as well as protect you. 'I don't think you can love me into safety,' she had said.

And then, from this angle and cold perspective, I imagined the two of them, Niemeyer and his daughter, in the dark water – this still-dangerous and to us unforgiven man who would eternally be that: a Magwitch and his daughter – struggling in the water that was rolling with noise, and heaving from the propeller of the ship that had abandoned them there. They cannot see each other, and he can barely feel her within his arms because of the cold. And breath . . . time is running out and they surface into the black air and inhale everything into themselves, gasp more breath in. All he must do is not let her go yet, this daughter he cannot see, can barely feel with his blunt fingers. But at least they are in the air now, on the surface, the skin of the Mediterranean, a hint of a moon, a hint of a light on a distant shore.

Niemeyer holds her face in his shackled hands, as he did for that final second on the deck rail to signal their departure. He puts his mouth on hers and she opens her mouth, and with her tongue she pushes the key that had been clenched in her teeth forward, into his keeping. They have difficulty holding on to each other, their bodies being tossed around, and in all that dark sea, the key is something too small and delicate to be passed from hand to hand. As the currents are strong, threatening to pull them apart, he will take the key *himself* from his mouth and attempt to release the lock. So now he lets go of the girl, lets go of the surface, and sinks with the key, alone, focused only on unlocking the padlock with his fingers that are already stiffening from the cold. This is the moment when he will or will not remain a prisoner for ever.

They have told her not to wait for him. She has sacrificed enough. Her father, if he is able to free himself, will follow and find her wherever she is. The historical ports are ringed around them. It is, after all, the great internal sea, discovered centuries ago and inhabited since, where ships navigated by stars, or by the temples on promontories when it was daylight. Piraeus, Carthage, Kuakas. All those coastal city-states of the Aegean, that were gateways for tribes who simply walked there

280

out of deserts or had swum to shore when their ships were wrecked by high winds in a storm. Asuntha moves away. She has posed for weeks in the profile of a person terrified of water. And now, all that held-back youth drives her forward. She lights out for whatever land will hide her until she is found. So that for now what she swims towards is just *somewhere* – to one of those ancient cities that was formed originally because of its existence on a delta or a reliable tide – to make a new life. As we too might do when we make our own landfall.

Niemeyer surfaces again for another breath, and in the darkness, in spite of the night wind, he hears the direction she is swimming in. He sees the *Oronsay* lit like a long brooch, far away, aimed towards Gibraltar. Then he sinks again, not yet free of his lock, whose small, subtle portal is hard for the key to find in this dark water and in the echo and whine of the departing liner's engines.

Letter to Cassius

FOR MOST OF MY LIFE I KNEW THERE WAS NOTHING I could give Cassius that would be of use to him. And during all these years I have never seriously imagined contacting him. Something about our relationship fulfilled itself during those twenty-one days on the ship. I felt no need (save for a slight curiosity) to know him more. The template of Cassius was clear, at least as far as I was concerned. I knew even then that he would be a self-contained creature, owing nothing. His only gesture outward, apart from our companionship, which was obviously just temporary, was the concern he had for that girl. And when Asuntha disappeared into the sea, I saw my friend, as if burned by an adult truth, retreat further.

An artist with burned hands. What was his life like after that? The last years of his teens must have been a time when he could rely on no one and believe in nothing. It is easy to be such a person when you are an adult, when you can survive on your own. But Cassius, I suspect, lost the rest of his childhood on the ship that night. I remember him standing there for ever, no longer beside us, searching the dark blue fluorescent wash.

I know that without all I have drawn from Ramadhin's quiet kindness, I would not think of going towards Cassius now. He has become a belligerent force in the art scene. There is easy mockery in him. But that doesn't matter. He had been a boy of twelve and had taken the step to protect someone with a childhood mercy. In spite of his almost natural anarchy he had wished to care for the girl. Strange. He wished to protect Niemeyer's daughter, as Ramadhin wished to protect Heather Cave. What happened that the three of us had a desire to protect others seemingly less secure than ourselves?

I thought at first that if I had a title, something like *Voyage of the Mynah*, I might reach him, wherever he was. For he would not know me by my real name. If I had reached Miss Lasqueti in her present home with my nickname, I might also reach him. I have no idea if Cassius reads, or if he scorns reading. In any case, this account is for him. For the other friend from my youth.

Arrival

WE SLIPPED INTO ENGLAND IN THE DARK. AFTER ALL
our time at sea, we were unable to witness our entrance into
the country. Just a pilot barge, blinking its blue light, was
waiting at the entrance of the estuary, and guided us alongside
a dark unknown shoreline into the Thames.

There was the sudden smell of land. When the dawn eventually lit whatever was around us, it seemed a humble place.
We saw no green riverbanks or famous cities or great spanning
bridges that might open up their two arcs to let us through.
Everything we were passing seemed a remnant from another
industrial time – jetties, saltings, the entrances to dredged
channels. We passed tankers and mooring buoys. We searched
for the heraldic ruins we had learned about, thousands of miles
away in a history class in Colombo. We saw a spire. Then we
were in a place full of names: Southend, Chapman Sands,
Blyth Sands, Lower Hope, Shornmead.

Our ship gave four short blasts, there was a pause, then
another blast, and we began to angle gently against the dock
at Tilbury. The *Oronsay*, which had been for weeks like a
great order around us, finally rested. Farther upriver, deeper

inland from this eastern cut of the Thames, were Greenwich, Richmond and Henley. But we stopped now, finished with engines.

As soon as I reached the foot of the gangplank I lost sight of Cassius and Ramadhin. A few seconds had passed and we were separated, lost from each other. There was no last glance or even realisation that this had happened. And after all the vast seas we were not able to find one another again in that unpainted terminal building on the Thames. Instead, we were making our way through the large crowd nervously, uncertain as to wherever it was that we were going.

A few hours earlier I had unrolled and put on my first pair of long trousers. I had put on socks that crowded my shoes. So I was walking awkwardly as we all descended the wide ramp down to the quay. I was trying to find who my mother was. There no longer remained any sure memory of what she looked like. I had one photograph, but that was at the bottom of my small suitcase.

It is only now I try to imagine that morning in Tilbury from my mother's perspective, searching for the son she had left in Colombo four or five years earlier, trying to imagine what *he* looked like, having been sent perhaps a recent black-and-white snapshot of him, to help identify one eleven-year-old in the horde of passengers coming off the boat. It must have been a hopeful or terrible moment, full of possibilities. How would he behave towards her? A courteous but private boy, or someone eager for affection. I see myself best, I suppose, through her eyes and through her needs as she searched the crowd, as I did, for something neither of us knew we were looking for, as if the other were as accidental as a number plucked from a pail who would then be an intimate partner for the next decade, even for the rest of our lives.

'Michael?'

I heard 'Michael,' and it was a voice scared of being wrong. I turned and saw no one I knew. A woman put her hand on my shoulder and said, 'Michael.' She fingered my cotton shirt and said, 'You must be cold, Michael.' I remember she said my name so many times. I was looking at first only at her hands, her dress, and when I saw her face, I knew it was her face.

I put my suitcase down, and I was holding her. It was true I was cold. I had been worried up to that moment only of being lost for ever. But now, because of what she said, I was cold. I put my arms around her and my hands were against her broad back. She leaned away and looked at me, smiling, and then moved forward to hold me tighter against herself. I could see part of the world to the side of her, the figures rushing past barely aware of me in my mother's arms, and the borrowed suitcase with all I owned beside me.

Then I saw Emily stride past in her white dress and, pausing, turn her head to look back at me. It was as if everything had stopped and reversed for a moment. Her face gave me a careful smile. Then she walked back and put her hands, her warm hands, over mine that were there on my mother's back. A gentle touch, then a deeper press, like some sort of signal. Then she walked away.

I thought she had said something.

'What did Emily say?' I asked my mother.

'Time to go to school, I think.'

From the distance, before she disappeared into the world, Emily waved.

Author's Note

Although the novel sometimes uses the colouring and locations of memoir and autobiography, *The Cat's Table* is fictional – from the captain and crew and all its passengers on the boat down to the narrator. And while there was a ship named the *Oronsay* (there were in fact several *Oronsay*s), the ship in the novel is an imagined rendering.

Acknowledgements and Credits

Robert Creeley for a stanza from his poem 'Echo'; a line by Kipling from 'The Sea and the Hills'; a verse by A. P. Herbert. A paragraph from Joseph Conrad's 'Youth', a passage by R. K. Narayan, and a line by Beckett about despair. The remark by Proust appears in a letter to René Blum, 1913. The lines from Jelly Roll Morton's 'Winin' Boy' appear in Alan Lomax's *Mister Jelly Roll* (1950). Other songs quoted, or referred to, are by Johnny Mercer, Hoagy Carmichael, Sidney Bechet and Jimmie Noone. Some information on Sidney Bechet is drawn from Whitney Balliet's wondrous *American Musicians II* (included is a quote by Richard Hadlock that appeared in the *San Francisco Examiner*). Thanks to *The Daily News,* Sri Lanka, for the germ of the 'Sir Hector' story that had its basis in a long-ago incident. The characters, names and dialogue in this novel however are pure invention, as is placing Sir Hector on a sea voyage. Material on triremes is drawn from *The Lords of the Sea* by John R. Hale. Eudora Welty wrote the two lines (quoted below) on embarcation in *The Optimist's Daughter.* Mr Mazappa's 'good book' is *The Maltese Falcon* by Dashiell Hammett. The scrawled lines in the Visitor's Book at Cassius' Art show were written by his friend, Warren Zevon, who was visiting from New Jersey.

Thanks

To Larry Schokman, Susie Schlesinger, Ellyn Toscano, Bob Racie, Laura Ferri, Simon Beaufoy, Anna Leube, Duncan Kenworthy, Beatrice Monti, Rick Simon, Coach House Press, Jet Fuel in Toronto, the Bancroft Library in Berkeley, California.

Also John Berger, Linda Spalding, Esta Spalding, Griffin Ondaatje, David Young, Gillian and Alwin Ratnayake, Ernest Macintyre – for the loan of a character, Anjalendran, Aparna Halpé, and Sanjaya Wijayakoon. To Stewart Blackler and Jeremy Bottle, as well as David Thomson some years later. And Joyce Marshall, who once smoked a cane chair.

Thank you to Ellen Levine, Steven Barclay, Tulin Valeri, Anna Jardine, Meagan Strimus, Jacqueline Reid, and Kelly Hill. Thanks to all at Knopf USA – Katherine Hourigan, Diana Coglianese, Lydia Buechler, Carol Carson and Pei Loi Koay. Many thanks to Louise Dennys and Sonny Mehta and Robin Robertson. A very special thank you to my Canadian editor and publisher Ellen Seligman.

For Stella, the sweet hunter – no more thunderstorms.

For Dennis Fonseka, *in memorium.*

'The boat came breasting out of the mist and in they stepped.
All new things in life were meant to come like that . . .'